ID0897939

The Nobbie Stories for Children and Adults

The Nobbie Stories for Children and Adults

By C. L. R. James

Edited and introduced by
Constance Webb
Foreword by Anna Grimshaw

University of Nebraska Press
Lincoln and London

© 2006 by the Board of Regents of the University
of Nebraska. All rights reserved. Manufactured in
the United States of America. ⊗

Book typeset and designed by Richard Eckersley
in Robert Slimbach's Adobe Minion fonts.

Library of Congress Cataloging-in-Publication Data
James, C. L. R. (Cyril Lionel Robert), 1901–
The Nobbie stories for children and adults / by
C. L. R. James; edited and introduced by Constance
Webb; foreword by Anna Grimshaw.
p. cm. ISBN-13: 978-0-8032-2608-1 (cloth: alk. paper)
ISBN-10: 0-8032-2608-X (cloth: alkaline paper)
1. James, C. L. R. James (Cyril Lionel Robert), 1901 –
Correspondence.   2. Authors, Trinidadian – 20th
century – Correspondence.   3. Children's stories –
Trinidadian and Tobagonian.   I. Webb, Constance.
II.Title.

PR9272.9.J35N63 2006   813'.52–dc22   2005026398

For C. L. R. James Jr.

Contents

Foreword

C. L. R. James was one of the outstanding figures of the twentieth century. A distinctive writer of fiction, short stories, and literary criticism; an astute commentator on cricket; an outstanding theorist and historian of revolution; and one of the leading figures of the Pan-African movement, James lived a long and remarkably full life. He was born in Trinidad in 1901. His father was a schoolteacher; his mother, whom he memorably describes in his semiautobiographical book *Beyond a Boundary*, passed on to her son her tremendous love of literature. James (or Nello as his mother called him) was educated at the island's premier educational institution, Queen's Royal College. Schooled by Oxford and Cambridge masters, his colonial education was founded upon the Greek and Latin classics, European literature, and British history; but from a precociously early age, to the exasperation of his father and teachers, James was determined to establish his own course in life. His childhood was dominated by two passions: books and cricket. By his early twenties he was a prominent member of a small circle of writers and intellectuals committed to exploring a new, authentically Caribbean subject matter. Before leaving for England in 1932, James published a number of short stories that celebrated the vitality of Trinidadian "backyard" life. One of these, "La Divina Pastora" (1927) was included in E. J. O'Brien's *Best Short Stories* that appeared in the following year.

James arrived in London with the intention of making his way as a writer of fiction. He carried with him the manuscript of a novel, later published as *Minty Alley* (1936). Within a few weeks of his arrival, however, he moved to Nelson, Lancashire, to stay with the well-known cricketer Learie Constantine. When he returned to London a year later, he quickly became caught up in the radical movements of the time, influenced by his experience of living in the industrial north of England. He immersed himself in the intense debates that raged on the Left about the Soviet Union, the possibilities for revolution in Europe, and the struggle of colonial peoples for emancipation. James was a striking figure in prewar London. He was over six feet tall, handsome, learned, and expertly schooled in the European intellectual tradition. He distinguished himself as a highly effective public speaker and ferocious debater. James moved easily between the different worlds of cricket, literature, and politics, forging critical relationships with a diverse range of people that included the publisher Leonard Woolf; George Padmore, who founded the International African Service Bureau and was later one of Kwame Nkrumah's closest advisers; and the distinguished African American singer Paul Robeson.

During his six years in England, James emerged as a leading writer and speaker on questions of revolutionary politics. His distinctive perspective emerged in three important books: *World Revolution* (1936), *The Black Jacobins* (1938), and *A History of Negro Revolt* (1938). Each of these works substantively challenged existing positions; and the originality of James's thinking about political leadership, the relationship between Europe and the colonies, and the significance of the Russian Revolution continues to stimulate contemporary debate and scholarship today.

In 1938 James accepted an invitation to address audiences across the United States on the situation in Europe. His speaking tour ended in Mexico where he met Trotsky and discussed with him matters concerning what was then known as the "Negro Question." James was enormously stimulated by America. He appreciated its vast landscape, unique history and culture, and distinctiveness from Europe. America became the site of some of his most important thinking. For over a decade, working with a handful of close collaborators, James sought to resolve a number of key problems in the theory and practice of revolutionary politics that he had identified in his publications of the 1930s and that had continued to plague the Left. The task he set himself was difficult and demanding. By the late 1940s, however, James and his circle had reached a new political position. It was articulated in a number of important works that included "The Revolutionary Answer to the Negro Question" (1948), *Notes on Dialectics* (1948), and *State Capitalism and World Revolution* (1950).

Significantly, James had pursued this work in conjunction with a profound engagement with American literature and popular culture. He was close to writers such as Richard Wright, Ralph Ellison, and Chester Himes. He developed a passion for the movies, often escaping to the cinema late at night and sometimes seeing the same Hollywood film many times; he eagerly embraced comic strips and radio soap operas, fascinated by the passionate following and lively involvement they generated among huge audiences. These aspects of American society prompted James to begin a very different kind of writing project than the one in which he had been engaged with his political collaborators. In *Notes on American Civilization* he argued that America was a distinctive civilization, indeed as one that advanced the European conception of civilization. James set himself against the prevailing view of intellectuals who had long disparaged America. But he was forced to abandon work on this manuscript in order to focus his energies on avoiding deportation from the United States. His original visa had expired many years earlier. By 1948 the Immigration and Naturalization Service had caught up with him and had begun proceedings to remove him from the country. James was interned on Ellis Island in 1952. Here he began working with some of the ideas from his unfinished *Notes on American Civilization* and completed a much shorter book on Herman Melville, *Mariners, Renegades, and Castaways* (1953). Melville was a key figure in James's understanding of modern society, and his reading of *Moby Dick* was boldly original. He sought to use his book – and his associated public-lecture series – to galvanize support for his case. He was not successful, and in 1953 James left the United States for England.

During the 1950s James wrote extensively on the new political movements that were unfolding in Europe (especially in Hungary), Africa, America, and the Caribbean. These movements brought his earlier writing on social and political upheaval into new focus. James's work increasingly addressed issues about nationhood, leadership, and popular democracy as the former colonial territories became independent and their new rulers struggled with problems of government. Many of these ideas found focus in his study of the resistance to British rule by people of the Gold Coast, *Nkrumah and the Ghana Revolution* (1966). James's understanding of the issues surrounding the transition of power was also importantly shaped by his own renewed experiences in the Caribbean. In 1958 after an absence of twenty-six years, James returned to Trinidad. The island was moving toward autonomy, and James threw himself whole-heartedly into local debate and mobilization. He edited the *Nation*, a newspaper dedicated to involving people in discussion about their political future. But James's time in the Caribbean was cut short by a growing disagreement with Eric Williams, a one-time close ally and the man poised to become Trinidad's first prime minister. On the eve of independence, James returned to England. A year later, in 1963, he published his semiautobiographical memoir, *Beyond a Boundary*, to great critical acclaim.

James continued to be a prolific writer and impressive public speaker until well into his eighties. During the 1960s and 1970s he published widely on a range of topics that included cricket, art and aesthetics, literature, politics, and history. He traveled extensively, visiting Africa and the Caribbean and returning to the United States. He held a number of positions at American universities and was actively sought out by a younger generation of activists. Given his peripatetic life, copies of James's works were often difficult to locate, but the publication of three volumes of his collected essays – *The Future in the Present* (1977), *Spheres of Existence* (1980), and *At the Rendezvous of Victory* (1984) – ensured that his ideas rapidly gained currency among new audiences. In 1981 he delivered a widely reviewed series of television lectures in Britain. Shortly afterward he decided to settle in London once again. Until 1984 he maintained an active speaking schedule. He also continued to write. *Cricket*, a collection of his essays and letters about the game, was published in 1986, and in the same year a major exhibition of his life and work was held at the Riverside Studios. During his last years, James received many visitors from across the world. He returned to many of his earliest passions – Mozart and Beethoven, Shakespeare and Thackeray, Michelangelo and Raphael – while at the same time remaining deeply engaged with events in the world. James died at home after a short illness in May 1989.

The Nobbie stories were written by James for his son, C. L. R. James Jr., nicknamed Nobbie, who was born in 1949. His mother, Constance Webb, had met James ten years earlier while he was on a speaking tour of the United States. Webb, a young white model and actress who was politically active in California, attended a talk entitled "The Negro Question" given by James in a Los Angeles church. In her memoir, *Not without Love*, Webb offers a striking description of this first encounter with James: "from the wings strode a six-foot-three-inch-tall, brown-skinned handsome man. His back was ramrod straight, his neck rather long, and he held his head slightly back, with chin lifted. There was an elegance and grace in his stance, and he looked like a prince or king. He was carrying books and an untidy sheaf of papers that he placed on the podium and never looked at again." At the end of the meeting, James and Webb were introduced. It marked the beginning of an extraordinary romance that was fueled by their very different experiences and trajectories.

James was captivated by Webb's beauty, vitality, independence, and expansive Californian personality. For him, she became a powerful symbol of America itself. The relationship between them – the passion, the struggles, the uncertainties, the moments of supreme happiness – was charted in the numerous letters that James wrote to Webb, published posthumously as *Special Delivery* (1996). Beginning shortly after their meeting in 1939, their correspondence spanned time and great distance. Although only James's letters have survived, they provide a unique insight into his developing courtship and life with Webb. Moreover, they tell a story that is not just confined to two people but one that illuminates – in remarkable ways – the world in which they lived.

In 1944 after five years of courtship, pursued mainly through letters, Webb moved from the West Coast to New York. Some two years later, she began living with James. They married in 1948, and a year later their son, Nobbie, was born. Already James was in difficulties with the Immigration and Naturalization Service. When he finally left for England, Nobbie was four years old. The stories that James wrote in the form of letters are a moving testament to his desire to remain closely in touch with the family he had left behind in America.

James began writing the Nobbie stories in 1953. Through his distinctive cast of characters – Good Boongko, Bad Boo-boo-loo, Moby Dick, Nicholas the Worker, and others – he explored questions of friendship, conflict, community, ethics, and power in ingenious and often humorous ways. Nobbie, too, is addressed by James as part of the Club and is given his own name, Chungko. The tone of the writing is light and playful, never patronizing. Although written for a child, it is interesting to trace how certain general preoccupations of James's come to be skillfully woven into *The Nobbie Stories*. Aside from a focus in particular letters on specific events and personalities that James was addressing in his other work of the time, we may also discern here the author's mature conception of politics as something inseparable from life itself and anchored in people's relationship with one another.

James was preeminently a *writer*. Over the course of his life, he experimented with a surprisingly diverse range of literary forms. He wrote essays, editorials, newspaper articles, polemic, political analysis, fiction, short stories, drama, and historical narrative. He was also a tireless correspondent. It was as a writer of letters that James was perhaps at his most inventive. Not only did he exchange ideas passionately on many different topics with many different correspondents, but he also creatively used the form itself to explore and inhabit very different subjectivities. This playfulness is one of the outstanding qualities of James's letters to Webb. It was central to his relationship with his son. The Nobbie stories are an expression of the imaginative, witty, curious, and profoundly human spirit that animated James's work. From the earliest short stories, James reveals himself to be an acute observer of character and situation, his writing manifesting an unusual empathy with people across disjunctions of class, race, gender, and generation. Fifty years after they were written, the Nobbie stories will continue to appeal to children and adults alike.

Anna Grimshaw

ACKNOWLEDGMENTS

To Antje Alexander, Natalia Ely, and Vivian Hall, whose concern and loving support made this book possible.

Introduction

These stories are absurd. Whoever heard of a club composed of people, animals, birds, lizards, two fleas, and even a whale? The Club is like a little democracy: everybody takes part in discussions, and both people and animals make suggestions. Sometimes they don't agree about how to solve a problem, but they work together until everyone is satisfied.

A father whose four-year-old son was wrenched from his arms by a deportation order that returned him to England after fifteen years in the United States wrote these stories.

The events taking place in the country were absurd. It was 1953; three years after Senator Joseph McCarthy had launched a crusade against national subversion. He charged that a large number of known communists were working in the State Department. Among those he attacked were Gen. George C. Marshall, a former secretary of state and a Nobel Peace Prize winner. He also charged the Roosevelt and Truman administrations with "twenty years of treason." He rolled over the country like a juggernaut and eventually included President Eisenhower's administration when he increased the number of years of treason to twenty-one. McCarthy's tactics involved personal attacks on individuals by means of widely publicized indiscriminate allegations based on unsubstantiated charges.

People were pilloried if there was the slightest hint that they were less than 100 percent in agreement with McCarthy's notion of what an American should be or do. People were urged to inform on family members, friends, associates, and neighbors. Those who would not were sent to jail or blackballed and unable to find work. Fear dominated the land; everyone became suspect.

Despite the fact that the father who wrote these stories detested communists and had written a book and articles against the Soviet Union, the judge handed down the order of deportation. He claimed that writers, particularly those possessing original ideas, were a danger to the country; they stirred things up.

Cyril Lionel Robert (C. L. R.) James, whom I called Nello, wrote these stories. Our son C. L. R. Jr., nicknamed Nobbie by his father, was four years old when Nello was deported. We agreed that he should leave of his own volition so that one day he could return to the United States. If the government carries out a deportation order, one is never permitted to enter the country again. We hoped that in a year or so McCarthy would be discredited and the atmosphere would change.

Nello and I had long talks about the future of our son and how to keep the father-son ties as close as possible despite the distance. He asked me to write every week and tell him everything that was happening to Nobbie and me. He wanted to know about any problems as well as good news. He in turn would also write every week. Since he had always told Nobbie stories, he would now write them down and send as often as he could. Nello said that he would use these stories not only to instruct but also to address any problems that were troubling his son.

So, exiled in London, Nello began to write stories that would teach his child important values – loyalty, honesty, integrity, courtesy, generosity, respect for fellow humans, and appreciation of the natural world, including animals, birds, fish, reptiles, even fleas. Nobbie's father believed that the Golden Rule was important for children to learn: *Do unto others, as you would have them do unto you.* Nobbie was also to learn about the arts – great literature from the Bible, the Greek myths, history, music, painting, architecture, and sculpture. Then there needed to be added a sense of community responsibility. To do this he placed the stories within the context of a club.

As a result of Nello's concerns, his stories are morality tales in the tradition of Grimm and Aesop. But they are so cleverly told, with sly humor, suspense, and sometimes absurdity, that good and evil behavior is disguised but not lost in the adventures of the protagonists, Good Boongko and Bad Boo-boo-loo. As you can tell by their names, one is a good boy and the other is a bad boy. Nevertheless they are friends maybe because sometimes Good Boongko does naughty things and Bad Boo-boo-loo does good things. As in real life, no one is perfect – neither all good nor all bad.

Good Boongko and Bad Boo-boo-loo have lots of adventures, some good and some dreadful. But everything turns out all right in the end. Some of these adventures take the boys into the realms of famous people, historic landmarks, sculpture, architecture, and Greek myth.

Bad Boo-boo-loo especially likes the Bible story of Daniel in the lion's den. He imagines his own club member and friend, Leo the Lion, in the same situation. What if his friend had *not* gotten a thorn in his foot? In the Coliseum would Leo have eaten Nicholas the Worker or Peter the Painter? It gives Boo the shivers to contemplate, but being ever curious and sometimes a little morbid, he likes to imagine what the outcome might be. In another story, with the help of a time machine, he is wafted to a gathering of knights and saves his hero, Sir Lancelot, from a critical situation.

On the other hand, Good Boongko has his favorites as well: Herodotus, who was called the Father of Lies; Roundheads and Cavaliers; and David and Goliath.

Bad Boo-boo-loo also secretly likes the tale of David and Goliath, but because his friend is so enthusiastic about it, he pretends indifference. But sometimes when he is alone, he dreams he is David and goes to a vacant lot to practice with his slingshot.

Mothers and fathers today will enjoy reading these stories to their children because they are educational yet filled with humor and human insight. The range is wide. They relate past and present and envision a hopeful future; at the same time they are playful and unique. The pet name salutations and closures have been retained because they add to the intimacy between father and child and may appeal to young readers – as if they are reading something secret.

The Nobbie stories were written more than fifty years ago. Many have been lost, and others are undated. To arrange the stories, I drew upon my memory of them, information found in accompanying letters, and any plot sequences connecting them. There may be errors in continuity, but because each story stands on its own, the sequence is inconsequential and does not interfere with a reader's pleasure.

1. Serial not Cereal

Before sailing to England Nello noticed that Nobbie did not have a full-length coat. He had a ski jacket and other warm tops, but they did not satisfy his father. I think, too, that he wanted to leave his son something special so he would think of his daddy every time he wore the coat. So we went shopping, and Nello was insistent that the lining be a light color. After we took the coat home, Nello put his finger to his lips, signaling me not to say anything. He then took the coat into the bedroom and was gone for about ten minutes. When he emerged he had a look of glee on his face and was holding the coat high in the air. Nobbie was intrigued, suspecting something unusual. Then Nello turned the coat inside out and said, "Voila." He had drawn in indelible ink a stick-figure picture of himself wearing glasses and holding a pipe in his mouth. "See Chungko-roo, whenever you wear your coat your daddy is right there with you, keeping you warm and loving you all the time." The following story was written almost immediately after Nello's arrival in London. The coat was still uppermost in his mind.

When we received this story, I was not sure that Nobbie would understand it. He was only four years old, and although very intelligent, the play on words and the humor at the end might be beyond his comprehension. I need not have been concerned because after I read it to him he wrote his father the following: "Daddy, I loved that story about the serial you sent me daddy. And the man who came to fix the aerial and he had so much confusion about the serial even you got confused. Remember daddy?"

Hi There Chungko:

How are you little boy? Do you feel very warm in your new coat, and every day you put it on, do you see your daddy with his glasses and his pipe in the picture on the inside of the coat? Here is a great big hug for you Chunkeroo, and by the way, man, you are not sending to tell me how you like the stories. I don't know if you like the story about the bad animals and how they got into the hole and were covered over by the net. The last installment that I was to send to you today was to tell you how Rhino was taking the letter in his ears to the other bad animals and how Nicholas the Worker, made Tweet-Tweet the Bird fly up in the trees to keep an eye on Rhino to see what he was doing. But Nob listen carefully to what I am saying. Let us for a moment forget this story. You have me little boy, you understand me? Let us for a moment forget the story about Rhino. I am going to tell you another story, the story about the Serial. And when I have told you this story about the Serial, then next time I shall finish the story about the bad animals. OK, Nob? OK. So now here's the story about Serial.

Now this story is about that bad boy Boo-boo-loo who was always doing bad things. One day in this country where Boo-boo-loo lived, Xmas was coming near. And all the people on the radio and owners of the big newspapers and the government municipality and everybody got together and decided to give a big prize to anybody who could guess, or rather who could work out, a certain word by a certain day. This word they had written down on a piece of paper and had sealed it up and put it away in the vault of a big bank. Nobody could get at it. And only two people knew – the president, who had chosen the word, and the secretary of the president, who had helped him choose it. So if you got this word right, you would be able to go to ten stores and choose three presents from each one, one for yourself and two for anybody you wanted to name. Now you could imagine what a wonderful prize that was, and all kinds of people wanted to find the correct word so that they could go to the store and choose the present for themselves and choose a present for their parents. And naturally Bad Boo-boo-loo heard of this competition and he wanted to take part in it.

Now you didn't have to guess the word altogether. The president said that he would give certain hints every now and then in the paper as to what the word was and he would give figures that you would have to add and subtract and these figures would tell you what the letters were and then these letters would enable you to guess what the word was. But Bad Boo-boo-loo first of all was very lazy. He didn't want to take all the trouble to get someone to read the paper for him every day to try to find out what this word was. But still he wanted to win the prize. So Bad Boo-boo-loo went to Philbert and Flibert the two fleas and told them to try to find out for him what the word was. Now Philbert and Flibert lived very quite retired lives. They didn't know anything about the competition. All that they knew was that Bad Boo-boo-loo had asked them to find out a word in a certain envelope. Now Philbert and Flibert could go anywhere. So they went through the keyhole of the bank and they went through the keyhole of the hall and they found a little spot in the envelope that wasn't thoroughly sealed down, and although Philbert couldn't read, Flibert was a reader and Flibert came back and told Bad Boo-boo-loo that the word in the envelope was *Serial*. Now when Bad Boo-boo-loo heard that he didn't stop to think at all. He said *Serial* must mean *cereal*, something that he used to have for breakfast every morning. So Bad Boo-boo-loo thought that he knew the word and he was sure to win the prize. So while everybody was very busy looking up in the paper and trying to guess what the word was, Bad Boo-boo-loo just walked around with a smile on his face because he was sure he was going to win. Then suddenly one day, the big shots who were organizing the competition said that when you found out the word you had to bring what the word represented. If you thought the word was *book*, you had to bring a book. And if you thought the word was *typewriter* you had to bring a typewriter. And if you thought the word was *cushion* you had to bring a cushion. And so forth. So Bad Boo-boo-loo went and bought a box of Rice Crispies. He said that's a cereal and he was sure he was going to win. So on the day of the competition a whole lot of people turned up in the stadium to see how the thing would go. A great number of people had given up trying because they felt that it was too hard to find one word. But Bad Boo-boo-loo was there with his box of cereal tied up in a paper. And when the master of ceremonies called Boo-boo-loo, Bad Boo-boo-loo came up and said in a loud voice "CEREAL" and started to open his parcel. Now when Bad Boo-boo-loo said "cereal" the president and the president's secretary opened their eyes and began to tell everybody around that the boy had won. The word was *Serial*. But when Bad Boo-boo-loo opened his parcel, they saw that instead of having a story in a lot of installments, he had Rice Crispies. Now, Chungko, you have to follow me very closely here for this story becomes very complicated. The president had said that Bad Boo-boo-loo had gotten the correct word. But the president meant *Serial*, a story in installments. But Bad Boo-boo-loo had misunderstood Philbert and Flibert and he had heard the word *Serial* and thought it meant some breakfast food. So when Bad Boo-boo-loo opened his parcel before the judges and was getting ready to go up for the prize, the president said, "That is not the *Serial*. It is another *serial*." So all the people who were around began to get very confused. Bad Boo-boo-loo said loudly: "If *cereal* is the word, here is my cereal."

The president said, "*Serial* is the word, but it is another kind of serial."

One of the other judges said, "This whole thing is very mysterial."

Whereupon the president lost his temper and said, "What kind of nonsense is that? You mean that the whole thing is very mysterious."

"Oh, yes," said the man, "I meant mysterious but all this talk about *Serial* made me say mysterial."

Now the president wanted to tell the man to be serious, but he was so confused with all this business about serial that he told the man, "I wish you would be serial."

The man got very mad and said, "What? You want me to be a breakfast food?"

But the president explained that all he wanted to say was that he wished the man would be serious. So the man became pacified and wanted to say to the president, "I wish you would be more careful in future."

But Chungko, do you know what he said? "I wish you would be more serial in future."

Now by this time the whole platform was in a tremendous confusion. Then a man came up to the president with a box in his hand

and they asked him what he wanted. And he said, "I want to see the aerial."

So thereupon everybody on the platform looked at the man and said to themselves, here is another mess about *Serial*. So they asked him again, "What do you want," and the man said he wanted to see the aerial.

By this time the president got so angry that he called some policemen to throw this man off the platform, but when the police came the man said, "I am an electrician. They told me that the radio and television sets up here are not working very well and that I should come and attend to the aerial. That's what I have come to see." And he said very slowly again, "I WANT TO SEE THE AERIAL." The president asked him, "So, Mr. Electrician, you have nothing to do with *Serial*?" The electrician replied with great scorn, "Cereal? Me? I can't stand the stuff."

The president had just got out of this and was wiping his forehead and wondering what he was going to do about Bad Boo-boo-loo when a young lady walked up to the platform and the president asked her who she was. She said, "I am misterial."

The president didn't want to lose his temper anymore so he said, "You mean, my dear young lady, that you are mysterious."

The young lady said, "Mr. President you insult me, I am a respectable young woman. There is nothing mysterious about me. I said I am misterial."

Whereupon the people on the platform all got very mad with the young lady. They all began to shout. "We have had enough of this mess about serial and misterial and aerial. Young lady you are guilty of a breach of the peace and coming here and making remarks about misterial." But the young lady with great dignity opened her purse and took out a card and said, "Here is my name. My father is Tom Terial, or as people call him, Mr. Terial, and my name is Mavis Terial, or as some people call me Miss Terial. That is Miss Jones over there. Over there is Miss Thompson, and I am Miss Terial. So what is all the fuss about?"

By this time the president was in an awful mess and he put his hand to his head and attempted to say, "All this is very mysterious." But by this time, all that he could say was, "All this is very mysterial." And here the poor man collapsed.

However, order was restored at last and it was decided to open the envelope and there they saw the word *Serial*. And they said whoever has got that word will gain the prize. And do you know who had worked it out, my dear Nob? Good Boongko. He had spent a lot of time looking up all the words in the paper and he had guessed it and he had a whole story all cut up in little pieces, and at the end of each piece Good Boongko had marked, "to be continued," so that he really had the word *Serial* and he brought the story for them to look at. So Good Boongko won the prize and all those present thought that Bad Boo-boo-loo had done a very bad thing in trying to get a prize by cheating.

November 13, 1953, London

2. The Bomb Threat – Part 1

Although the hydrogen bomb explosion in the Marshall Islands had been announced in March by President Eisenhower, some people were still talking about it in December because it exceeded all estimates of its power. Whether Nobbie had heard about the bomb earlier I don't know because he gave no indication that he had. However, he came home one day from school troubled. Someone had told him that it was a bad bomb, and if evil people got hold of it, everyone would be dead. I immediately called Nello to tell him about Nobbie's fears, and he promised a story in the next mail. This story and the next reassured our son.

My dear Choong-ko,

Here is a story about our old friend, Bad Boo-boo-loo, that boy who was always doing bad things, and the Club.

It was a few days before Christmas, and Bruno the Bulldog, sent out a letter saying that all of them should come to a meeting because there was a bad situation in the world, and they had to do something. So that day everybody came, and of course, old Bruno was chairman. He sat at the front and looked around the room to see how many members were present.

There was Good Boongko over in one corner; there was Lizzie the Lizard, talking to Tweet-Tweet the Bird. Peter the Painter, was there, with his beard; and in the back of the room there was Storky the Stork talking to Leo the Lion; and then there were the twin fleas, Philbert and his twin brother Flibert. In fact, the only person who was not there was Moby Dick, and nobody could blame Moby Dick because he sent a message to say that he was in the water and had to stay there; but Moby said he wished them well, and if they wanted him to do anything, they only had to send and let him know.

So Big Bruno in his big voice called the meeting to order and they called a roll of those present; but when they came to Bad Boo-boo-loo's name, he wasn't there, so they called "Bad Boo-boo-loo!" but there was no answer. So there it was; for this most important meeting Bad Boo-boo-loo, who was always doing bad things, was not present.

They asked Good Boongko if he knew where Bad Boo-boo-loo was, but Good Boongko said, "No," but that he had called Bad Boo-boo-loo on the phone just before he left and his ma said that Bad Boo-boo-loo had gone for a little walk and then was going to the meeting. So Peter the Painter got very angry and said that they should move a vote of censure against Bad Boo-boo-loo for not coming to this important meeting. But Big Bruno said that the best thing to do was to wait and hear what Bad Boo-boo-loo had to say.

Then Big Bruno stood up and explained why he had called the meeting. He said "Members of the Club, I have a friend who knows a lot of things, and he tells me that he has heard about a plot to destroy the world with a big bomb. There are some monsters up in the sky who are very good at making bombs, and they have formed a league with some evil people down in the world here, and these people have agreed with the monsters that they should drop some bombs in special places and create a lot of confusion and disorder down here in the world, and when this takes place, then the evil men down in the world will be ready to seize the world and do what they like with it." Big Bruno stopped speaking for a second to see how everyone was reacting to the bad news. "So, my friends," said Big Bruno, "that is the rumor I have heard, and I believe that the best thing we could do is to have a meeting and talk it over."

So the meeting began, and they talked, but Big Bruno couldn't give them any real facts; all he could say was that he had heard about it. That was the situation at the meeting when suddenly there was a knock at the door and Bad Boo-boo-loo walked in, and in his hands he held a big box. When Boo-boo-loo came in, some of the members began to say, "Where have you come from? You should have been here before – you are that bad boy who is always doing bad things," but Big Bruno hit the table very hard with his paw and said, "Silence – Order, please!"

Everybody kept order and Big Bruno asked Bad Boo-boo-loo to speak up. Bad Boo-boo-loo said, "I was coming to the meeting when I saw a wild duck having a fight with an eagle by the side of the road. The duck was quite tired out and he was on the ground. The eagle was about to stab the duck with his beak, so I picked up a stick and hit the eagle so hard that he had to fly off. Then I picked up the duck and I had to take him and give him a bath, and something to eat, because he was very tired and wounded."

Peter the Painter shouted out, "I don't believe that story!" So Bad Boo-boo-loo jumped on top of a table and opened the box he was carrying and said, "Here is the duck," and there, in truth, was a large wild duck.

So now there was a lot of confusion in the room, as you can imagine Nob, but the wild duck stood up, and he said, "Quack, quack, quack, listen to me please." He was so serious that everybody listened and this is what he said: "This boy Bad Boo-boo-loo," said the wild duck, "is speaking the truth. I was having a fight with an eagle who wanted to kill me. I am a wild duck, and I and my friends fly very, very high in the air, and we heard some monster up in the sky talking to one another about a plot to destroy the earth. My brother and I flew up closer to hear. We had heard nearly everything when they saw us, and they came after us, to kill us so that we should not tell anyone. I do not know what happened to my brother, but I fought with that eagle all the time, and he would have killed me if Bad Boo-boo-loo hadn't come to my assistance."

Now, Choongko, my boy, you can imagine the sensation! Big Bruno told the wild duck, "You are the very person we wanted to see, because we had heard the rumor about the plots, but we didn't know who were the monsters and who were their friends down in the world below." The wild duck said, "I know them all!" The people in the meeting were very glad and they appointed a committee to go and tell the chief of police about the plot, but when they went to tell the chief of police, the wild duck said, "He is one of the evil men who is in the plot." The chief of police chased them away; he said it was all nonsense. So there they were; they knew what was happening, but they could not get anybody to believe them, and they had only a few days. In the next installment I will tell you what happened.

December 20, 1954, London

3. The Bomb Threat – Part 2

You will remember, dear Chung-ko that the last story told about Quack-Quack the Duck rescued by Bad Boo-boo-loo, and the plot by some monsters.

The question now, my dear Choong-ko, was how to prevent the monsters up above from carrying out their plot with the bad men on earth. Nobody knew what to do. So Big Bruno said, "I have some friends, some old friends of mine, whom I visited when I paid a visit to Europe many years ago; the only trouble is I don't know how to get in touch with them now." So Bad Boo-boo-loo, who was always one to talk up, said, "Who are these people Big Bruno?" And here my dear Nob, you have to look at the pictures I sent you, and some I am sending you today. Big Bruno said, "In Florence there is a castle and at the top of the castle there is a tower, and at the top of the tower there is a little man," and here Big Bruno dug down into his briefcase, which he used to carry around his neck, and showed them the picture. And my dear Nob, if you look at the picture, you will see the little man at the top of the tower. Then Big Bruno said, "I have another friend who lives at the top of the Eiffel Tower," and he showed them the picture. Then Big Bruno said, "In Marseilles there is a statue of David, and that statue is my good friend also."

"Where did that statue of David come from," asked Bad Boo-boo-loo. "There is no time for that now," said Big Bruno. "I will tell you another time, but if you look at the map, you will see that if I could only communicate with the little man in Florence, and the other man at the top of the Eiffel Tower, and the statue in Marseilles, we will have the whole continent covered, for those are the three most important points."

Suddenly, Quack-Quack the Duck, whom Bad Boo-boo-loo had brought, said, "I know those places well; the only trouble is I am wounded, but if I could only get there, I know them because whenever I flew to Europe, high up in the air, I always went to see them and used to talk to them."

Then Nicholas the Worker said, "OK, let us ask Moby Dick to take Quack-Quack by sea, and when they reach those countries, Quack-Quack will only have to fly right up to the top of the buildings and give the message."

"That is a good idea," said Big Bruno, and they all rushed out to the beach, where Moby Dick was having a snooze. When they reached Moby Dick, they told him about the monsters and what they planned to do, and he said he was ready. But Quack-Quack said he did not want to go alone; he wanted somebody to go with him, so they asked him whom he wanted. Quack-Quack said, "Bad Boo-boo-loo, because he found me." Well, they did not want Bad Boo-boo-loo to go, but he said he would behave well, and Moby Dick said, "OK, let him come." And so Moby Dick sailed off across the sea with Quack-Quack and Bad Boo-boo-loo holding tight on to his back.

My boy, in no time they were on the coast of Italy, and Quack-

Quack went up and told the little man at the top of the tower in Florence. Then they rushed off to Marseilles and told the statue of David. Then they rushed off to the north coast of France and told the man on top of the Eiffel Tower.

Nob, my boy, those three fellows, they wasted no time. They said, "We have to let people know; we're not going to let these bad people get away with it." So what they did was this: the little man in Florence started sending out flashes to the man on the Eiffel Tower, and the man on the Eiffel Tower sent the flashes to the statue of David, and the statue of David sent flashes back to the man in Florence, so that all the people in Europe saw these flashes going round and round, and they came out into the streets to ask what was going on up there. Everywhere, where the people saw the flashes, they came out, and soon there were millions and millions of people out in the streets asking what was wrong. Then some people went up to the towers and asked, and the little men and the statue told them. The people then went and looked for the bad men and found them and dragged them out, and they were so frightened when they saw all the people that they confessed how they had plotted. The people took them and put them away in jail, where they could not do any mischief. Then the man on the tower in Florence, the one on the Eiffel Tower, and the statue of David sent up messages to the bad men up in space and told them that it was no use their trying any schemes because their bad friends down below had been found out. So those evil spacemen up there got frightened and did not do a thing.

Meanwhile, Moby Dick had stayed near the coast with Quack-Quack and Bad Boo-boo-loo watching what had happened, and when the situation was safe, Moby Dick said, "Well, it is time to get back now; those at home must be very anxious." So Moby Dick took them fast through the water, and soon they were back home again and they gave the good news.

Well, Choong-ko, everybody agreed that Quack-Quack should become a member of the Club, and Quack-Quack said he was very happy to be a member, only he was frequently flying about all over the world. Everybody was pleased with Bad Boo-boo-loo also, and Bad Boo-boo-loo asked only for one reward. He said, "I want to know all about the statue of David." "OK," said Big Bruno, "I will tell you about it another time," and Bad Boo-boo-loo was so sleepy that he said, "OK, when I see you next time, Big Bruno, you will tell me about that statue of David."

So that is the end of the story Choong-ko, and next week I will send you another one.

December 27, 1954, London

4. Michelangelo and the Statue of David

Although many of the stories are in response to interests or problems revolving around different social relations and situations facing his son growing up in a racist atmosphere, Nello often wove Bible stories, myths, and history into the narrative. He believed a child was never too young to learn about great art, music, and literature. Placing them within the magical context of the Club, where Good Boongko and Bad Boo-boo-loo and other members could interact, brought them to a level a child could understand.

Hello, Choong-ko!

I promised to tell you the story about the statue of David by Michelangelo. Bad Boo-boo-loo, when he came back from the trip with Moby Dick to Europe, wanted to know about this statue. You remember he had seen the statue in Marseilles, and the statue had helped them. Also, you have a picture of the statue. And now, Choonk, I have seen that statue, and I hope one day you will see it, and read about it.

Nicholas the Worker had promised to tell Bad Boo-boo-loo the story, but Good Boongko, who could read, went to the library and got a book about Michelangelo, and he read the story, and he told it to Bad Boo-boo-loo one afternoon.

Michelangelo was a sculptor: he used to make statues, and he lived in Florence, which is in Italy – you know, the one shaped like a boot. Well, Italy was a republic; so when Good Boongko said that it was a republic, Bad Boo-boo-loo said, "What is a republic?" So Good Boongko tried to explain, but although Good Boongko could read, there were many things he used to read that he could not understand. That happens to everyone who is just learning to read. So they went off to Nicholas the Worker to find out what was a republic. So Nicholas thought a long time, and then he said, "Well, you see Good Boongko and Bad Boo-boo-loo, we have a club, and in that club Big Bruno is the chairman, and he conducts the meetings; he is the leader, and we listen to him, but Big Bruno cannot tell us to do what he wants us to do if we do not want to do it. Every member of the Club can say what he likes in a meeting. Big Bruno has to listen and then we all decide what we want to do after everybody has said what he wants to say. That is a republic, where everybody can talk and discuss and do what they think they want to do. Do you understand that Bad Boo-boo-loo?" Bad Boo-boo-loo said, "Yes," but, said he, "what is *not* a republic?" So Nicholas the Worker thought a little bit, and he said – his face very serious – "Sometimes, Bad Boo-boo-loo, there is a nice club, and everybody likes it, but the president gets a lot of police and bad men with guns and then he doesn't allow anybody to say anything, and he says what must be done, and everybody has to do it." "Huh!" said Bad Boo-boo-loo, "if I was in a club and they tried to do that, I would leave," and Nicholas the Worker shook his head and said, "Sometimes you cannot leave; anyway, you two boys run away and leave me, I am busy."

So Good Boongko and Bad Boo-boo-loo went away, but Good Boongko was very happy. He said, "Now I understand about Michelangelo better than before." "Go on," said Bad Boo-boo-loo, "tell me." So Good Boongko continued, "The town of Florence was a republic, and Michelangelo loved the republic, but a lot of bad men wanted to smash up the republic and force everybody to do just what they wanted. So the people were very mad at this, and everybody was giving what he could to help in the fight against these bad men; some were coming ready to fight with swords, others were giving money, and others were building up the walls to make them strong. Others were bringing food to store up to help feed the people if there was a siege; and everybody was getting ready." "Okay," said Bad Boo-boo-loo, "but what has all this to do with Michelangelo and the statue?" Good Boongko told him, "Do not be impatient, you just listen. Michelangelo wanted to give something to help, or to do something, and finally he made this big statue of David, and to the people Michelangelo said, 'Just as David fought for the Israelites against Goliath and the Philistines, so everyone today must fight like David against these horrible Goliaths who want to smash our fine republic,'" and, my dear Choongko, when all the people saw this fine statue of David and they remembered how David had fought against Goliath, they all felt ready to fight to the last drop of blood for the republic. And the president of Florence said, "Some people have given money and the young men have joined the army, and some people have brought food, but Michelangelo, with this statue, has really given a fine gift to the republic," and said Good Boongko, "That is how that statue was made, and a lot of people everywhere love that statue, and the people of Marseilles had a copy made so they could see it every day in their own country." And, my boy, pretty soon other countries made copies so they could always remember David and his fight against the bad people who wanted to destroy the republic of Florence.

Bad Boo-boo-loo said, "Michelangelo gave a statue to help in the defense of the republic; I never heard of a thing like that before." And then, at the next meeting a strange thing happened. Big Bruno was in the chair and Bad Boo-boo-loo jumped up and said he wanted to say something, and Bad Boo-boo-loo made a speech. This is what he said: "Our club is a republic, and everyone can say what he likes and we must defend this club. David slew Goliath and Michelangelo made a statue of David to help defend the republic of Florence. I propose that Peter the Painter make a picture of David to put up in our club to help to defend our republic." Big Bruno, as you know, Nob, was very serious and had a big voice. But this time he said, "Bad Boo-boo-loo, you come up here near to me," and Bad Boo-boo-loo went up near to Big Bruno, and Big Bruno said, "You made a fine speech, that is a good proposal. I hope all of us will always be ready to defend our little republic, and I want everybody to know that although Bad Boo-boo-loo does many bad things, yet he sometimes does some good ones." And there was a lot of cheering and merriment, and they all took Bad Boo-boo-loo off to the Italian restaurant and gave him a fine big feed of noodles and Pepsi-Cola.

January 17, 1955, London

5. The Dirty Snowball and White Raincoat

Despite the magical world Nello created, the stories relate to the real world in which children grow up. Questions of truth and dishonesty, good and evil – in other words, morality – are key components of the narratives. In this story an accident occurs and although sincere apologies are proffered, the vain victim of a minor incident is unjust and takes out his anger on Bad Boo-boo-loo.

How are you, my dear Choongo?

I hope you are well. I have been laughing for the last three days at a story concerning Bad Boo-boo-loo and Big Bruno the Bulldog. Bad Boo-boo-loo was playing in the park when Good Boongko, Leo the Lion, Nicholas the Worker, and the others were having a snowball fight.

Now the keeper of the park was a very funny man, and to tell you the truth, Choongko, Bad Boo-boo-loo had thrown some snowballs in the park, and the keeper had threatened to put him out. But this day Bad Boo-boo-loo threw a snowball at Nicholas the Worker. Nicholas ducked, and the snowball hit the keeper, who was passing by, right in the center of his tummy. The keeper was not only a cantankerous man, but he was a very vain man; he used to like to wear a white raincoat. This snowball happened to be muddy, and it made an awful mess of the raincoat. The keeper got mad, and he said that

Bad Boo-boo-loo was to leave the park and not to come back. Bad Boo-boo-loo and the others apologized and asked his pardon. He said, "No" and that Bad Boo-boo-loo hit him with the snowball purposely. He said, "Bad Boo-boo-loo was to go out and stay out." So out poor Bad Boo-boo-loo had to go, and the next day, when the others went into the park to play, poor Bad Boo-boo-loo had to stay out. When Big Bruno heard of this he said, "We will fix that park keeper." So the next day Big Bruno the Bulldog went and stood up by the gate where the keeper used to come into the park. It was very wet and dirty there, and Big Bruno told Bad Boo-boo-loo to stand up near to him. Soon they saw the keeper coming wearing his nice white raincoat.

Now, Choongko, you know how a dog goes into water and then shakes himself and the water splashes all around? As soon as the keeper was near, Big Bruno went into a pool of water, and as soon as the keeper was passing him, Big Bruno jumped out of the water and shook himself. From his head down to his feet the keeper was plastered with mud and water. Big Bruno simply ran off while Bad Boo-boo-loo stood up there and asked the keeper, "Please, Mr. Keeper, may I help you?" The keeper was raging mad because a lot of people were laughing, but he could not do anything, so he shouted at Bad Boo-boo-loo, who was standing near to the pool of water. He thought very quickly, and he said, "All right little boy, you can come back in the park to play, but be careful how you throw your snowballs." And after that, Choongko, Bad Boo-boo-loo played in the park all the time with the others, and no more accidents happened to the keeper.

Okay, Choongko, that is the story this time, and I would be glad if you tell me what you would like a story on next time.

January 21, 1955

6. Mighty Mouse and the Conceited Cowboy

Nobbie came home from playschool one afternoon and said that some of the boys had been making fun of another child by calling him Shrimp. He was the smallest in the class. I asked him if he joined in the attack, and he said, no, because the boy was crying. I explained that size had to do with one's parents; that is, usually tall parents had tall children and short people had short children. "Well," said Nobbie, "I am the tallest in the whole class!" He sounded a little smug. After thinking about the conversation, and Nobbie's reaction, I wrote Nello about the episode. A week later he sent the following story.

Well, my dear Choongko, how are you today, little boy?

Here is a story about an old friend of ours whom we haven't heard anything about for a long time. You know, just outside the town where Bad Boo-boo-loo and Good Boongko lived, there was a huge prairie and on the prairie was a ranch where there were many cows and bulls and horses, and the cowboys there used to hold rodeos. So, there was one cowboy who was six foot tall – a very big and strong fellow – and he always used to win all the events; but particularly, he could ride very wild horses and very wild bulls without falling off.

Now, Choongko, there was nothing bad about one cowboy winning all the events, but this cowboy, because he used to win, got very conceited, and he used to walk around with his hands in his pockets sneering at everybody, and one day when he was walking along the street, he saw Bad Boo-boo-loo and Good Boongko in front of him, and he gave one of them a push with his right hand and the other one a push with his left hand and said, "Get out of the way, you little brats." So, he was so offensive that a lot of people began to say that it was necessary to find some cowboy to beat him at the rodeo. That was the only thing to make him learn to behave. Well, some folks got together, and they sent to this world where we live and asked the Lone Ranger and Cisco Kid to come to give this ill-bred cowboy a good beating.

Well, Choongko, on the day appointed, Cisco Kid and Lone Ranger were there ready. The first thing, the big cowboy comes up smoking a cigarette with his hands in his pockets. "Huh!" he said, "Lone Ranger and Cisco Kid, they are nothing." So the Lone Ranger got up on the bad bull to ride him and that bad bull started kicking, and in one minute the Lone Ranger was down in the mud. The big cowboy laughed and said, "I told you so." So the grooms came out and took the bad bull in, and after a few minutes they brought him out. "Your turn now, Cisco Kid," said the tall cowboy. Cisco Kid went up on the bull's back, and whoosh, in one minute the bull had kicked up so hard that the Cisco Kid was down in the mud too. "Hee, hee, hee, hee," laughed the tall cowboy. "So that's your famous Cisco Kid." Then they brought out the bull again and the tall cowboy got up on his back, and although the bull kicked up and made a fuss, the tall cowboy was able to control him, and ride him, and then tame him, and everybody said, "The tall cowboy is really the best cowboy that ever was."

Now, Bad Boo-boo-loo did not like this at all, and one day, at a club meeting Bad Boo-boo-loo said, "I know what we ought to do; we ought to send for Mighty Mouse." Everybody agreed, and Nicholas the Worker, who knew a lot about sending messages into space, sent up a message to Mighty Mouse, who was busy among the planets. So Mighty Mouse came down through the air with his long cape trailing behind him – our old friend Mighty Mouse, Choongko, who could always be depended upon in an emergency. So they told Mighty Mouse what was happening, and Mighty Mouse said, "Okay, let us arrange a rodeo." Mighty Mouse disguised himself as a cowboy, and a new rodeo was arranged. But when they brought out the bull, Mighty Mouse said, "Big Cowboy, you ride him first." The big cowboy said, "No, no, you ride him." But Mighty Mouse said, "Ladies and Gentlemen, I am the visitor and he is the great cowboy, let him ride first." So everyone said, "That is right cowboy, you get up," because they were all fed up with the mean way that big cowboy used to behave. So the big cowboy had to go up, and my dear Choongko, as soon as he got up on the bull that bull kicked up so wildly, down came big cowboy in the mud. Everybody was pleased, but they were a little nervous. So Mighty Mouse then turned to Lone Ranger and Cisco Kid, who were standing up watching, and said, "Would you like to have a try at him now?" "Sure," said the Lone Ranger, and he got up on the bull, and when they let it out of the gate, he rode it and controlled it, and tamed it; you should have seen the miserable face on the big cowboy. Then Cisco Kid got up on the bull, and he rode it, and controlled it, and tamed it. Everybody was so glad and Bad Boo-boo-loo and Good Boongko were there clapping and cheering like mad. Then Mighty Mouse held up his hand, and he called the grooms who used to prepare the bull for riding. Everybody was silent. "Come on," he said to them, "I know what is happening. Confess." The grooms held their heads down and confessed. Big cowboy had bribed them to put sharp spurs in the ears of the bull whenever someone else was going to ride him, and that had made the bull so mad that it was impossible to control him, and so it was that big cowboy could always win.

So when everything was over and Mighty Mouse was about to leave, Bad Boo-boo-loo asked him, "But, Mighty Mouse, *how did you know that?*" Mighty Mouse said, "My boy, I've known the Lone Ranger and the Cisco Kid a long, long time, and when I heard that there was a bull that they could not ride, I said to myself, 'I am sure someone is playing tricks with that bull.' So when I came in, I examined what the grooms were doing, and I soon found out."

Well, Choong-ko, the big cowboy was so ashamed that he became the quietest and most humble cowboy that they had ever seen, and one day, when Bad Boo-boo-loo and Good Boongko were walking in the street, and he was striding past, he said "Excuse me my young friends," and Bad Boo-boo-loo and Good Boongko stood aside for him to pass. He was a very humble cowboy indeed. But Bad Boo-boo-loo spent a long time asking himself, "Why is it that we should have had to send for Mighty Mouse to work out this problem? We should have been able to work it out for ourselves."

ok, Choonk, 'til next time.

January 25, 1955, London

7. Emperor Jones and the African Drums

When Nobbie was only a few months old, Nello claimed he was not going to force his political beliefs on his son: "We will let him make up his own mind," he vowed. However, this story, simple as it is, embodies Nello's political and philosophical beliefs: people will always rebel against tyranny, and ordinary human beings are resourceful and intelligent.

Boom! Boom! Boom! That is the way the African drums sound in the forest, and this is the story of Bad Boo-boo-loo, Good Boongko, Emperor Jones, and the African drums.

I am afraid, Choongko, that Bad Boo-boo-loo still keeps on doing bad things sometimes. This day, he and Good Boongko went down by the river, and they saw a boat there. Now Bad Boo-boo-loo's mother had told him never to get into boats unless the boatman was there, but Bad Boo-boo-loo not only went in but also managed to get Good Boongko to come in too because the boat was tied to a stake on the shore by a rope.

But as soon as they got into the boat, the rope slipped and off they went down the river. The current took them out to sea, a strong wind began to blow, and on they went, on and on and on, out of sight of land. They were in a terrible spot because they might have been lost at sea. But after many hours they came to an island and the boat went near the shore. So they jumped out and scrambled onto the land.

There the first thing they saw was an African beating a drum. He wasn't beating it loud, but he sat beating it quietly to himself as if he was practicing. So Bad Boo-boo-loo went up to him and told him what had happened to them and said he was hungry. So the man gave Bad Boo-boo-loo and Good Boongko a coconut each and went on beating his drum. Bad Boo-boo-loo ate the coconut, and he began to feel that he wanted to get back home.

So he asked the man how they could get right back to where they had come from, and the man said that he could not think about that now, because there was going to be a big affair on the island that night. "Tell us about it," said Bad Boo-boo-loo. The man was still beating his drum, but he was beating it very quietly, and Bad Boo-boo-loo could hear what he had to say.

What the man said was this: he said that on that island they had had a fine republic. Everybody was getting on fine, but then one day a big African came there on a boat and he had some very good guns and weapons. He won over some of the Africans; he made himself a dictator – a boss over everybody else. Nobody could say what he wanted to say, and this bad fellow called himself an emperor. He said his name was Emperor Jones. He was an awful tyrant, and now all the people were fed up with him and they had decided to get rid of him that night.

"How are you going to do that?" said Bad Boo-boo-loo. The African replied, "We are going to use the drums on him." "Use the drums on him?" said Bad Boo-boo-loo. "How are you going to do that?" "If you want, you can come with me and see," said the African. "Okay," said Bad Boo-boo-loo.

Choongko, my dear boy, that night the African gave Bad Boo-boo-loo a little drum, and he gave Good Boongko another little drum, and he told them to come with him and to do what he did. So the African started beating the drum quietly, and Bad Boo-boo-loo and Good Boongko were beating their drums quietly too.

They began to go through the forest, but soon all through the forest they began to hear drums beating, all around, African drums beating, boom, boom, boom, boom!

Soon the African told them to stop, and he climbed up into a tree. Bad Boo-boo-loo and Good Boongko climbed up behind him, and from the top of the tree, they could see a big house with some soldiers around it. "That is the house of Emperor Jones," said the African. "Where's the emperor?" asked Bad Boo-boo-loo. "He is inside," said the African, "but we're going to bring him out."

So they came down from the tree, and then the African began to beat the drum loud, and suddenly it seemed that the whole forest was nothing else but drums, all around, down in the grass, halfway up the trees, in the tops of the trees – only African drums, boom, boom, boom, boom! Choongko, the drumming was terrific.

Soon Emperor Jones – he was a big fellow – came out with a lot of pistols in his belt, and he and his soldiers rushed into the woods to look for the drummers. They were rushing straight to the African and to Bad Boo-boo-loo and to Good Boongko, but as soon as they saw him coming, the African stopped drumming and Bad Boo-boo-loo and Good Boongko stopped drumming too. But at the same time as they stopped, the drumming over on the other side of the forest grew louder and louder. So the emperor and his soldiers turned round and ran to where the drumming was loudest, but as soon as Emperor Jones reached the other side, the African, Bad Boo-boo-loo, and Good Boongko started drumming as hard as they could. The emperor rushed back, but by this time the African, Bad Boo-boo-loo, and Good Boongko had rushed off to another part of the forest.

All night this drumming continued, and Emperor Jones rushed from place to place, until at last in the morning he fell down exhausted. His soldiers ran away, and the Africans came out of the forest and took him prisoner. They took away his guns, and he begged pardon for his crimes against the republic.

So the republic was restored and Emperor Jones was put on a boat and told to go find himself somewhere else to live. But when the African told the people how well Bad Boo-boo-loo and Good Boongko had beaten the drums, they gave them a special boat to take them back home.

Now, Choongko, the end of the story is very funny because Bad Boo-boo-loo's mommy was very angry that Bad Boo-boo-loo had gone and stayed away the whole night. She said she had been very scared, and when Bad Boo-boo-loo turned up, he wasn't sorry for the fact that he had given so much trouble but started telling how he had beaten the African drums in order to defeat Emperor Jones and get the republic back for the Africans. But his mommy took Bad Boo-boo-loo on her knee and spanked him as hard as he had spanked the drums. But Good Boongko, who was very sorry that he had caused his mommy so much trouble – and said so as soon as he came back and promised not to do it again – was pardoned.

So that is the story of the African drums, my dear Choonk.

February 23, 1955, London

8. Nobbie's Birthday

The intention of this story, enclosed with a birthday card, was to make Nobbie feel included in the imaginary tales Nello was sending. Names of the Club's members were printed on the card. The picture referred to is one Nello often drew of himself, an oval with eyeglasses, dots for a nose, and a pipe jutting out from his mouth. Unfortunately, the card was lost.

My Dear Choongko,

Imagine what happened at the Club a few days ago. Mighty Mouse was coming through from the world in which we live, and he happened to visit the Club when a meeting was going on.

Mighty Mouse knows everything. And he told them of how there was a little boy named Nobbie and how his daddy called him Choongko and how this little boy's daddy used to write to him a lot of stories about the Club. The club members were quite astonished.

"So is that little boy," Bad Boo-boo-loo asked, "a little boy? Ho! We must write him a letter." Big Bruno, who was in the chair, said, "Oh, don't bother with that. That is only Bad Boo-boo-loo's foolishness. That boy is always doing bad things."

So Mighty Mouse said, "Well, I don't know about a letter. But I know his birthday is on April the fourth, so you can send him a birthday card." Then Bad Boo-boo-loo absolutely took charge. He asked Mighty Mouse, "You mean that little boy, Nob, knows about all of us?" "Yes," said Mighty Mouse. "Okay," said Bad Boo-boo-loo, "we'll send him a card from all of us."

So he got a big piece of paper and there they are. At the top is Big Bruno in the chair, and when Big Bruno is in the chair, he wears his glasses. And then one by one, Peter the Painter drew the pictures. That little boy Bad Boo-boo-loo, said, "Don't put any names. If he really knows us, he will recognize us." Nicholas the Worker said he would sign his name, and he signed in a fine strong writing. Good Boongko printed his name. But Bad Boo-boo-loo, he hadn't learned to write, so they had to mark his name in pencil and then he went over it in ink. You can see that Bad Boo-boo-loo was not a good writer.

But that boy Bad Boo-boo-loo, my dear Choonk, was up to a lot of tricks. After the card was made, Bad Boo-boo-loo went home and got his daddy to write a special message to the little boy. And Bad Boo-boo-loo didn't call the boy Nob. He called him Choongk. And you know what that rascal did afterwards? He said, "Maybe I don't write so well, but I am going to make a picture of what that little boy looks like." And then he made a lot of decorations around his own name, so that as soon as you look at the picture, you see Bad Boo-boo-loo's name first. That boy, Bad Boo-boo-loo, really, it is impossible to keep him quiet.

Anyway, Choongko, this is the card that the Club made. And you will see that Peter the Painter, after listening to a description of Nob's daddy by Mighty Mouse, made a picture of him, and it is a pretty good picture. Ask Mommy if she thinks it is a good likeness.

OK? Choonk.

Daddy

March 30, 1955, London

9. The Teacher Who Feared Rats

In a letter to his father, Nobbie defended Bad Boo-boo-loo, saying that he was not always doing bad things. This story was received soon after his father read Nobbie's letter. For the first time, Good Boongko is shown to be only human, and Boo is not the only one to misbehave.

My Dear Choongko,

I have a rather strange story to tell you this morning: it's about that boy Good Boongko. You know that Good Boongko is a good boy – in fact that is why he was called Good Boongko – and that Bad Boo-boo-loo was the boy who was always doing bad things. Well, this time Good Boongko did a bad thing. It was not very bad, but I will let you judge for yourself.

Bad Boo-boo-loo and Good Boongko went to the same school and were in the same class. There was a teacher there who was doing his best to get Boo-boo-loo to learn to read and write; he was a good teacher and he was a nice man, but he was afraid of rats.

Now many people are very brave when it comes to lions and tigers, but they are afraid of rats, and this teacher was afraid of rats, and mice too. One day when the class was outside at the back of the school where there was a train, a rat ran out from it, and this teacher got very scared and called upon the children to run away from that bad spot. From this, and from other things that they heard, all the children knew that he couldn't stand rats.

Now I don't know what got into Good Boongko's head, but one day he was passing along the street and there was a man selling a lot of mechanical toys: the man used to screw them up and they would run all along the pavement, little horses, little dogs, little elephants, and so on. And among these mechanical toys there were three large-size rats! As the rat is a rodent of different sizes, the maker of the toys had made them pretty big. Good Boongko bought the three of them and he took them home and put them in his cupboard. Why he bought them, Choongko, nobody can say: these things often happen to people – they just get a sudden idea in their heads and they do some bad and some foolish things. Good Boongko used to play with the rats in his room. Now, you must remember this: that he would not allow Bad Boo-boo-loo to see them. He said to himself, "If Bad Boo-boo-loo sees them, he is sure going to borrow them to take to school and scare the teacher." Now Good Boongko had no intention of using the rats to frighten the teacher. But one morning Good Boongko just put the three rats in his bag and went off to school with them. Why he did that, no one knows. Later poor Boongko couldn't say why he had done it, but he just had a feeling that he wanted to take the rats to school.

So that day he sat in class and this good teacher was talking to them. Suddenly Good Boongko's hand began to itch and without knowing what he was doing he screwed up the three rats; then he took one out of his pocket and put it on the floor, and the rat ran straight for the teacher. My dear Choongko, it was terrible, and it was funny too. The teacher jumped from his chair and went to one corner of the room. Good Boongko took out the other rat and sent it flying to the same corner of the room where the teacher was cowering. The teacher turned and jumped on the table, and that boy Good Boongko put another rat on one end of the table, and upon this the teacher turned and ran out of the room altogether.

There was a terrible uproar; some of the kids were frightened, but others were laughing, and then the head teacher came in and asked what was going on. Of course, when the head teacher came in, everyone was very quiet. The teacher stood behind the head teacher, looking very nervous and wiping his face with his handkerchief. The head teacher went and picked up the three mechanical rats, which were now quite still, and everybody started to laugh, but Good Boongko by this time was terribly frightened when he realized what he had done. "Who is responsible for this?" said the head teacher, and now Choongko, something very funny happened. Everybody turned and looked at Bad Boo-boo-loo because everybody felt that only Bad Boo-boo-loo would pull a trick like that, but Bad Boo-boo-loo this time was innocent. When everybody was looking at him, he jumped up and said with great indignation, "What are you all looking at me for, I didn't do a thing," so the head teacher said, "Are you sure, Bad Boo-boo-loo?"

Now if there was one thing Bad Boo-boo-loo was always ready to do was to speak up, and he said, "No sir, I didn't do it, I didn't do it at all; I brought no rats here." Then the head teacher said, "Then who was it?" And then, to the surprise of everyone, Good Boongko stood up and said in a weak voice, "I did it." "You did it, Good

Boongko?" said the teacher. "Impossible, Good Boongko would never do a thing like that," but Good Boongko said, "Yes, I did it, and I don't know why I did it, and I am very sorry." And although he tried hard not to, Good Boongko started to cry. You can imagine the sensation in the class. The teacher said to the head teacher, "Well, if it is Good Boongko who did that, let us forget it because he has always been a good boy," and everybody was so astonished at Good Boongko behaving in that way that they said nothing, and the whole affair passed off quietly.

But there were two things that happened. First of all – the teacher who was afraid of rats wasn't afraid of rats any more; he said that he was quite cured of those foolish fears, and it was a fact that on this point he became quite changed. The second point was that Bad Boo-boo-loo went about telling everybody that henceforth his name was Good Boo-boo-loo, instead of Bad Boo-boo-loo, and he kept on calling Good Boongko Bad Boongko. He would not stop it, day after day, but very soon he was in trouble again, but that I will have to leave for next time.

April 4, 1954, London

10. Androcles and the Lion

Despite his separation from Nobbie, Nello was concerned with his education and the moral questions children face when growing up in society. As a result, stories from the Bible, myths, literature, and history remain closely integrated with the world in which Nobbie lived. In this story it is clear that arrogance and impertinence are very bad traits for one to have and, ultimately, make one look very foolish indeed.

Hello, my dear Choongko:

I hope you liked the story of how Good Boongko got into trouble and how Bad Boo-boo-loo made bad jokes at him and called him Bad Boongko. To tell the truth, Nob, I laughed at that story very much myself.

Now I want to tell you another story – about Leo the Lion and how Bad Boo-boo-loo talked too much and got sat upon by Nicholas the Worker. One day Leo the Lion was listening to everybody telling stories and Leo said that when he was a little boy – I mean to say when he was a little lion – his parents used to tell him about the strange adventures of a lion who lived long long ago. This lion, it seemed, was running in the forest one day when a huge piece of wood with a sharp point got stuck in his foot, and he couldn't get it out; he was in great pain, and after a time the foot started to get bad. So he was limping around in the forest, and one day he saw a man walking. This lion started to go up to the man to show him his foot and to ask him for some help, but as soon as the man saw the lion, he was afraid, and he climbed up a tree. So the lion sat down at the bottom of the tree and he looked up at the man very pitifully, and he showed him his foot with the piece of wood stuck in it. So the man looked at the lion's foot, and he wanted to help him, but he was afraid of the lion; so he stayed up in the tree; he didn't know what to do.

Now, Choongko, by this time everybody in the Club was listening spellbound to this story that Leo the Lion was telling. It just fascinated them. So Leo the Lion continued with his story. The man was up in the tree half the day, and the lion remained down below, looking up at him until at last the man summoned up courage and came down. As soon as he touched the ground, he ran off at a great speed; but the lion did not run after him; he was so disappointed that he stretched out on the ground, and he put his head between his legs and started to cry. The man ran off a long distance, looking back to see if the lion was going to chase him, but the lion did not chase him and remained lying down under the tree. So it seemed that the man began to get curious as to why this lion was behaving in this peaceful way. Little by little he started to come back, and the lion remained lying on the ground. The man came nearer and nearer, and the lion lifted up his paw and showed it to him with the big piece of wood stuck into it, and it was all swollen and festered. So the man overcame his fears and walked up to the lion and took his paw in his hand. He saw all what was wrong and he held on to the piece of wood and he pulled it out. Then he tore a piece off his shirt and he bound up the lion's foot and began to walk towards the river telling the lion to follow him. The lion followed him. The man bathed his foot and tied it up with a cloth again, and told the lion goodbye.

Bad Boo-boo-loo began to say something, "But how . . ." As soon as Bad Boo-boo-loo said that, Nicholas the Worker said, "Keep quiet, Bad Boo-boo-loo, and let Leo go on." So Leo went on with his story. The lion got better, and one day some men in the forest captured him. They didn't kill him, but they took him away in a cage. They carried him to a big city where there were a lot of people and then they put him in an underground cavern and they didn't feed him for days. He got terribly hungry. Well, one day when he was raging with hunger, they let him out of the cage. He trotted out into a big open space surrounded by a lot of people shouting and cheering. He looked around and there were three other lions like him, all looking very hungry and very mad. Then, in the distance, they saw four men, and each lion began to rush at a man to eat him. So this lion reached his man first, and he was about to spring on him when he saw that it was his old friend who had helped him get rid of the piece of wood out of his paw. He stopped and walked up to him and said hello by lying down at his feet, and the man recognized him, and he stroked his head and they had a big hug. Everybody was astonished, and the other three lions, instead of eating the other three men, came up to this lion and said – in lion language of course – "Hi, what is going on here?" So the four lions sat down next to the four men and the lion told the other lions the story of how this man had helped him when his foot was bad, and the man told the other men. So that the eight of them were sitting down out there, talking and laughing away, and then a strange thing happened. Somebody came and told the men and the lions to follow him, and the men followed him, and the lions went behind, and they led them out of this place to the high road and then told them to go away and do what they liked. So after spending a little time together, they said goodbye, and the men went one way and the four lions went back into the forest, and everything was fine.

Androcles and the Lion 29

Well, my dear Choongko, all the members of the Club were listening to the strange story that Leo the Lion had told them. Leo said that his parents told him the story, and his parents had been told the story by their parents, and so the story had descended from parents to children for many generations, and the whole thing happened a long time ago.

Now that Bad Boo-boo-loo jumped up. He said, "I don't believe that story. All the lions were very hungry and they would have eaten up the men, and in any case, what is all this about a big open space where there were a lot of people, and a whole lot of stuff like that?" So Leo the Lion said, "I can't tell you any more than I have told you, but all of us little lions knew that story, and I believe it is true." "I don't believe it!" said Bad Boo-boo-loo, and Leo the Lion began to look rather angry. Then Nicholas the Worker intervened. He said, "The story is absolutely true." "How do you know that?" said Bad Boo-boo-loo. Nicholas the Worker said, "I will tell you, you impertinent young scoundrel. Many hundreds of years ago," continued Nicholas, "the Romans used to catch animals and starve them, and then they all used to gather on a big day and let loose the animals on men they did not like, and have a lot of fun watching the animals eat them. The Romans were very cruel people. The big open space that Leo the Lion referred to was called an arena, and round about the arena the Romans had a lot of seats in a huge stand. They called that stand the Coliseum.

"Well, the Roman writers say that one day they put a man called Androcles in the arena for the lions to eat him, but instead of the lion eating him, he went up to the man and began to play with him, and when all the people saw that, they asked Androcles what had happened. Androcles told them, and the people were so impressed that they let Androcles go free, and they let the lion go free also. And that," said Nicholas, "is the same story that Leo the Lion's parents used to tell him, and that is why I believe it is true."

Okay, Choongko, everybody was most interested in this, and Leo the Lion was very pleased because he said that these writings of the Romans that Nicholas the Worker had read confirmed the truth of the story his parents had told him.

Choongko, you know how Bad Boo-boo-loo liked to carry on. He started grumbling to himself that the whole thing sounded very funny to him, and so on and so forth. But Leo the Lion scored a wonderful point on Bad Boo-boo-loo. He said, "My dear Bad Boo-boo-loo, if you don't believe my story, ask Nicholas to lend you the book so that you can read it for yourself." And at this the whole Club started to laugh because everybody knew that Bad Boo-boo-loo couldn't read.

So that, my dear Choongko, is the story of Androcles and the lion.

April 13, 1955

11. The Club Starts a Newspaper

Two or three members of the Club, including Big Bruno, were angry because the local newspaper was unresponsive to their critical letters and articles. Bad Boo-boo-loo suggested that the Club write its own paper. His suggestion was accepted, but the article by Boo caused dissension. We know that Bad Boo-boo-loo always has an overwhelming need to feel important, but in this instance, is he right or wrong?

Here is the story about the newspaper and the Club and Bad Boo-boo-loo.

One day Big Bruno the Bulldog came into the Club in a great rage. He said that he wanted to bring to the attention of everybody a scandalous article in the newspapers about bulldogs and the way they barked and made a noise and disturbed people. Big Bruno said that it wasn't true because he had gone round and asked all his brother bulldogs and they had told him that only a few had done that. But this is what had made Big Bruno mad.

He had gone to Nicholas the Worker and they had written a letter to the newspaper saying that what the newspaper had said was not true. But the editor had refused to print it. Then Peter the Painter said that he too had written a letter to the editor about painters, but he had written five hundred words and the editor had only printed fifty and that had spoiled his letter. So everybody was pretty mad at this injustice. But nobody knew what to do until Bad Boo-boo-loo said, "Why not let us have our own paper?" At this, Peter the Painter said, "That would be fine but it is too difficult to print a paper, and after you print it, you have to dispatch it everywhere." Then Storky the Stork said, "I don't know about printing the paper, but if you have to dispatch it anywhere, I can take part of it." And as Storky said that, Tim the Eagle said, "If Storky the Stork can take some of the papers one place, I can take some of them another place." Then Nicholas the Worker said, "I have a little printing press at home, but it needs a lot of power to print the sheets." So Leo the Lion said, "Power? You mean to drive those machines? I can drive a machine for a whole day and not get tired." So Nicholas the Worker said, "Well, if everybody is prepared to do something, I believe we can have a paper."

Now between us, Choongko, when Bad Boo-boo-loo had made the proposal about a paper, he said it half in joke. But now the Club decided to have its own paper and Bad Boo-boo-loo got all excited. He said he wanted to write an article in the paper first thing. "But you can't write," said Tweet-Tweet the Bird. "Oh, yeah?" said Bad Boo-boo-loo, "I can dictate it and my mommy will take it down on her typewriter." So they decided they would have the paper and everybody would write articles and send them to Nicholas the Worker, who was the editor.

Boy, they got down to work. They called the paper FREEDOM because they said whatever anybody wanted to write in it could go in. They were still mad at the editor. So they organized the first issue. Leo went to the house of Nicholas the Worker and he tried out his big strong paws on the machine and said, "I can make it go." Peter the Painter drew pictures and everybody was busy writing articles and dictating articles and Good Boongko wrote a story for the paper and Storky the Stork and Tim the Eagle set their alarm clocks to be up early on Saturday morning so as to take the paper everywhere, and everything was set.

That was the situation and everything was ready except the article by Bad Boo-boo-loo. At the last minute Bad Boo-boo-loo came rushing in with two sheets of typewritten paper. He took the sheets to Nicholas the Worker who read them and started to laugh. But when he was finished, he was laughing still but he said, "I don't think that we should print this article." "What?" said Bad Boo-boo-loo, "not print my article? You have to print my article. Our paper is called FREEDOM and we all agreed that everybody should get his article printed. What is wrong with my article that you can't print it?" Then Nicholas the Worker read the article for everybody to hear. And do you know what that boy Bad Boo-boo-loo had done, that boy who was always doing bad things? He had written an article saying that the time had come to have a change in the Club and instead of Big Bruno being the president, he, Bad Boo-boo-loo, should be the president and preside at the meetings. When Peter the Painter heard that, he got real angry and said, "This is absurd. This troublesome boy Bad Boo-boo-loo wants to be the president and not only that, he goes and writes this for the first issue of the paper!" Bad Boo-boo-loo answered, "You said, all of you, that the paper was FREEDOM and everybody could write in it what he wants and would like to be printed, and I have written that for the paper and you have to print it."

Boy, Choongko, there was a real crisis. Nicholas the Worker said they had to have a special meeting and they sent off quickly for Big Bruno and everybody else to have a meeting to decide. Should they print the article of Bad Boo-boo-loo's or not? So next time, Choongko, I shall tell you what happened.

April 22, 1955, London

12. Bruno and Leo Have a Fight

One of our friends, James T. Farrell, the author of the Studs Lonigan trilogy and other books, loved to argue especially when he'd been drinking, which was often. Nello never argued; he discussed a topic. Farrell would hold forth about some author or literary subject, often vigorously. Nello would then say, "Is that so?" and gracefully move to another topic. Later, I'd ask him why he hadn't demolished Farrell's premise, and he'd reply, "It isn't cricket." That phrase is as important to the English as the Ten Commandments are to Americans. In this story, Nello wanted to instill in his son the concept that even when one is right, insisting on one's point of view when it might create problems or embarrass someone is wrong.

My dear Choongko,

As I was telling you last time, Nicholas the Worker said they had to have a meeting to decide about the article written by Bad Boo-boo-loo. They sent for Big Bruno, and as soon as he came, the meeting was called to order. Big Bruno said, "Well, the first thing we have to do is to hear the article." So Peter the Painter said, "Let Bad Boo-boo-loo read it because it is his article." Peter the Painter was only being spiteful because he knew that Bad Boo-boo-loo could not read. So Nicholas the Worker said, "I will read it for Bad Boo-boo-loo," and he stood up and read it.

Now, Choongko, this is the article that Bad Boo-boo-loo had written for the paper:

"We are having a paper, and this is my article for the paper. I believe the Club should have a change in the officers. Mind you, I don't want to say that Big Bruno isn't a good chairman: I think Big Bruno is a very good chairman, but I think we ought to have a change. I want to speak the truth. I, Bad Boo-boo-loo, I am only a little fellow, it is true, but I think I would like to be chairman sometimes. I wouldn't like to be chairman for long, but only for two or three meetings, and of course while I am chairman, Big Bruno would sit with the other members of the Club. My mommy, who is typing this article for me, has asked me why I want to be chairman. I don't know exactly why I want to be chairman, perhaps it's because I am just tired of sitting in the back here. My mommy has asked me again if I have anything new to propose as chairman. I don't know yet, but maybe when I am chairman, I shall find something new. At any rate, I just want to be chairman for a little while.

"I don't think I have anything else to say, so I had better stop. OK, that's the article by me, Bad Boo-boo-loo."

(Signed Bad Boo-boo-loo)

So Choongko that was the article that Bad Boo-boo-loo had written.

When it was read, everybody looked at Big Bruno, and Big Bruno said, "That is a ridiculous letter. Bad Boo-boo-loo will make us all look stupid if we publish this letter." Then a strange thing happened. Leo the Lion said, "Big Bruno, I believe you have to publish this letter by Bad Boo-boo-loo. You promised. So you have to keep your promise." "Don't talk nonsense, Leo," said Big Bruno. Leo the Lion said, "Don't you talk to me in that way, Big Bruno." And, Choongko, before you knew where you were, the two of them started a fight in the clubroom. Everybody got very excited and rushed to part them. But they kept on fighting and it was very hard to separate them. But in the end Nicholas the Worker took Leo the Lion home, and Peter the Painter took Big Bruno home. But that didn't stop them fighting. Leo the Lion called up Big Bruno on the telephone and said, "If you want to fight, come in the forest, and I will fight you there." And Big Bruno arranged with him to go into the forest that very night. So they went into the forest and they started to fight. Leo the Lion was strong. But Big Bruno was very experienced, and he sidestepped a big rush by Leo the Lion and hit him an awful whack just behind the ear, and Leo the Lion rolled over. "Serves you right," said Big Bruno and he set off home. He thought that Leo the Lion was going to get up soon after he had recovered.

But that is not what happened. There were some lion hunters in the forest looking for lions, and they had been looking all day and they hadn't got any. Now, as they were nearing home, they saw Leo the Lion lying down in the forest knocked out. So they threw their nets around him and made poor Leo prisoner and took him off to a camp in the woods.

Now Tweet-Tweet the Bird had seen Big Bruno and Leo go into the forest and he arrived just in time to see the lion hunters carry off Leo the Lion to the camp in the woods. So he went there and marked the place and then rushed off to the telephone and called up Big Bruno.

"Big Bruno," he said, "the hunters have captured Leo the Lion and they are going to kill him." Now by this time, Big Bruno was thoroughly ashamed that he had got into this fight with Leo the Lion, and when he heard this news from Tweet-Tweet, he called up the members of the Club and they all set out to go to the woods to find Leo in this camp. But just as they reached near the woods, they saw Leo walking slowly along with his head low down and his tail between his legs. Big Bruno rushed up to him.

"Leo, my dear fellow," he said, "we heard you had been captured and were coming to look for you. We are glad you escaped." "I didn't escape," said Leo. "One of the hunters started talking about Peter the Painter and I said I knew him, and when he heard that, he told the others to let me go. So here I am." "I feel pretty stupid about this whole thing," said Big Bruno. "I have behaved like an idiot." "And I, too, have behaved like an idiot," said Leo the Lion. "What were we fighting about?" said Leo. "For the life of me, I can't remember," said Big Bruno. Then Nicholas the Worker said, "You can't remember? It was that idiotic article that Bad Boo-boo-loo wrote for the paper." But here Bad Boo-boo-loo, who was feeling pretty scared, shouted out, "Forget my article. I don't want my article printed any more. Leave it out. It is a foolish article." But Big Bruno said, "No sir, we are going to publish that article and everybody is going to see that you want to be chairman. What do you say, Leo the Lion?" And Leo the Lion said, "This is a foolish fight and all on account of Bad Boo-boo-loo's nonsensical article. We are going to print it."

Now, by this time, Bad Boo-boo-loo was begging everybody to help him to keep the article out of the paper. But everybody said no, they were going to teach Bad Boo-boo-loo a lesson, and into the paper went his article. The result, Choongko, was that everybody who read the paper laughed at Bad Boo-boo-loo and the teachers and the little boys and everybody, including his daddy, called him "Chairman Bad Boo-boo-loo" for a long time.

I tell you, Choongko, Bad Boo-boo-loo didn't write another article for the paper for many a long time. Okay, Choongko.

April 27, 1955, London

13. Bad Boo-boo-loo Messes Up the Time

This is one of my favorite stories because it is magical. Imagine that the hands of a clock can talk and complain about their jobs; that is, one of the hands is unhappy and feels unfairly treated. Along comes Bad Boo-boo-loo, who thinks he knows everything and highhandedly tries to solve the problem. The moral is you should not complain about your job until you know how your labor contributes to the organization's functioning. And as for Boo, he should stop giving advice when he knows nothing about what is required and can't even tell time. As a result of his vanity and ignorance, a community falls into disarray.

Hi, Choongko,

I hear that you are going to the very big school in September. That I think is going to be a fine time, lots of new things to learn and new people to see. Already this is May. September is not far off, my boy. You must be all excited about it. Well, we must have patience when big and nice things are waiting for us in the future. Patience. That is a fine thing to have. And now for a story that made me laugh a great deal and I hope it will make you laugh too.

That boy, Bad Boo-boo-loo was passing by the cathedral one day when he saw some workmen coming out and talking about how they had gone up to the top of the tower where there was a big clock and how they would go back up there to work after lunch. Into the cathedral walks Master Bad Boo-boo-loo. He sees that the staircase by which the men went up and down is open and he walks up and up and up until he finds himself on the little balcony outside the clock. Just as he reaches up there, he hears Longhand talking to Shorthand. Longhand said, "I have to go round and round twelve times in twelve hours. And you, Shorthand, in twelve hours you go round only once. I am doing most of the work on this clock, and yet when the workmen come to give us food, they give you the same amount of oil that they give me. That shouldn't be. I should get more." Bad Boo-boo-loo was astonished to hear this. But he was even more astonished when he heard Shorthand say, "Longhand, I think you are right, but I don't know what to do. I wish we had somebody to advise us."

Choongko, you could imagine. As soon as that boy, Bad Boo-boo-loo, heard this, he says, "Oh, you all want somebody to advise you? I can advise you." So both Longhand and Shorthand said, "We are very pleased to hear this. What do you advise?" Bad Boo-boo-loo said, "Longhand and Shorthand, each of you just go round together. When Longhand moves from one number to another, Shorthand moves from one number to another. No more and no less. That is equality." "Thank you, little boy," said both Longhand and Shorthand. "That is what we will do." Now, Choonk, from that day on the big clock was always in disorder. The workmen fixed it, the engineers fixed it, and then the bishop fixed it. They sent for electricians. But however they fixed the clock, as soon as they went away, Longhand and Shorthand were always going at the same pace. This meant that the time was always wrong and a lot of people who used to do their work and set their clocks by the cathedral were always wrong and there was a general mess.

Now, Good Boongko was a smart boy, and he noticed that whenever they were going to school, Bad Boo-boo-loo would look up at the clock and laugh. And when Good Boongko heard all the trouble that the clock was giving, he said to himself, "Bad Boo-boo-loo has something to do with this." So one day he walked up the staircase and went out on the balcony. And sure as day he heard Longhand

and Shorthand talking of how they were following the advice of that bright little boy who had come up to see them one day. Good Boongko was very disturbed. "You all should not listen to that boy," he said. "He was just talking like that." But Longhand and Shorthand said, "No, we are very satisfied." Here Good Boongko hit on a plan. That afternoon he invited Bad Boo-boo-loo to go up with him to the clock top. And as soon as they reached up to the top, Good Boongko said, "By the way, Bad Boo-boo-loo, what is the time?" Now, Choongko, Bad Boo-boo-loo didn't know how to tell the time. Boy, he was in a mess. He tried to guess, but it was obvious that he couldn't tell the time. So Good Boongko said, "You don't know the time." And Bad Boo-boo-loo said, shamefacedly, "I am learning, but I don't know the time yet." When Longhand and Shorthand heard this, they got really mad. They said, "We don't care how stupid he is but we are clock people, and if it is one thing we insist upon, it is that people who talk to us know the time." Boy, Bad Boo-boo-loo felt pretty awful, and he and Good Boongko came down from the clock top. But Longhand and Shorthand said that they were not going to follow the advice of that little boy any more. Longhand began to go right round once every hour and Shorthand did his little piece from number to number every hour. The time was correct and everything went smooth. Only Bad Boo-boo-loo said to himself, "I am really a dumb one. If I had only known the time, they would have listened to me." OK, Choonk, that's it.

May 24, 1955, London

14. The Ghost at the Window

Nobbie wrote his father saying, "Daddy, I want you to send me a story next time about something dangerous and about a ghost and a witch and very spooky." The following story was to have a sequel, but one was not written. After reading the first episode, Nobbie did not want to hear anything more about ghosts and skeletons and wrote his father asking him not to send any more scary stories. And yet, a short time later, he wrote, "Dear Daddy, I loved the program, Richard the III. Richard III killed the children, two children in the tower. And he drowned another man and killed him. He wanted to be king but at the end he became dead."

Well, Choongko, don't be frightened now; keep a steady head, because this is the spooky story that you asked for – the story with the witch and the ghost, and as I told you, the skeleton. It happened to that boy Bad Boo-boo-loo.

There was an old lady who lived in a little house along the side of the road where Bad Boo-boo-loo used to pass to go to school. She was very old and she was very bent, and she walked with a stick.

Now Bad Boo-boo-loo was not a bad boy; as you know, Choongko, he was always doing bad things it is true, but he was not a bad boy. But he was careless, and he wasn't thoughtful enough about other people. So one day, when he was passing in the street with Good Boongko, they were playing ball, and Bad Boo-boo-loo threw the ball and it hit the old lady. Now what Bad Boo-boo-loo should have done was to go up to her and say that he was sorry, but he didn't do that. As soon as he saw that the ball had hit her, he turned and ran away.

Choongko, that old lady was a witch and she never forgave anybody who did her anything. That night, as Bad Boo-boo-loo lay in bed fast asleep, he heard a knocking at his window, and when he opened his eyes, there, just outside the window, was a terrible looking ghost dressed all in white, with the face of a skeleton, and through the white clothes you could see the bones of the skeleton. It was terrible.

Now Choonk, Bad Boo-boo-loo was a brave little boy; there it was, midnight, and he was alone in his room. Outside was dark, but behind the window was this skeleton in the white clothes of a ghost. "Oh, that's a lot of nonsense," said Bad Boo-boo-loo. "I am just dreaming, that's all," and he turned his face to the wall and he pulled the bedclothes over his head; but between us, Choonk, he was just a little bit frightened. But Bad Boo-boo-loo would not look again for a long time, but he heard three knocks on the window, knock, knock, and knock. He looked again, and there the ghost was, and this time its eyes were like balls of fire. Bad Boo-boo-loo was really scared, but he kept his head. "Nobody is going to frighten me," said Bad Boo-boo-loo, so what he did was to knock on the wall and to call "Mommy, come here a little, please." As soon as his mommy heard him call out, she came in, but as soon as she came the skeleton disappeared. Bad Boo-boo-loo kept a level head. Boo said to himself, "I am not going to tell them about this ghost, because there is no ghost there for them to see – they will think I'm just crazy." So when his mommy came in, Bad Boo-boo-loo said, "Mommy, I am sorry to call you, but I got up and I felt a little lonely." His mommy said, "That's all right, Boo," and she gave him a hug and a kiss and went back to bed. Bad Boo-boo-loo listened and he looked, but he saw nothing else.

Next morning Bad Boo-boo-loo rushed off to meet Good Boongko to go to school. "Boongko," he said, "I have something to tell you." "And I have something to tell you," said Good Boongko. Good Boongko was a very polite little boy, so he told Bad Boo-boo-loo, "You tell me your story first, Boo-boo-loo." Bad Boo-boo-loo told him all about the ghost. Good Boongko listened with his eyes wide open, and then he said, "You know, Boo-boo-loo, that's exactly what happened to me last night." "This is most astonishing," said Bad Boo-boo-loo, and Good Boongko echoed him, "Most astonishing."

Both of them agreed to say nothing for the time being, but that night was a Friday night, and Bad Boo-boo-loo got permission to spend the night at the house of Good Boongko, and to sleep with him in his room. They made up their minds to sit up and watch. Boy, sure as ever, at midnight they heard the knock on the window, and there they saw the skeleton, and this time it had long nails on each finger and the nails were sharp and pointed and a blue fire burnt at the end of them, and the eyes of the ghost were blazing red, and through the white clothes you could see the bones of the skel-

The Ghost at the Window 41

eton, and the ghost knocked on the window, knock, knock, knock. But those two little boys refused to be scared. They said, "What do you want?" The ghost said nothing but only knocked on the window, knock, knock, knock. Bad Boo-boo-loo and Good Boongko got out of bed and went to the window and said, "Go away, you can't frighten us." But then, that ghost, by some mysterious means opened the window and stepped into the room. This time Bad Boo-boo-loo got frightened, and he screamed out, "Mommy, Mommy!" Boo was so scared he forgot that he was staying in Boongko's house and his mommy was blocks away.

Now, Choongko, here I must stop. If you like the story you must send and tell me so, and I will go on, but it's a very spooky story, and I don't want to go on unless you tell me to do so.

So there, for the time being, we shall stop. OK, Choonk, send and tell me at once, and as soon as I hear from you, I shall send the second part. Boy, it's most frightening!

June 7, 1955, London

15. Police Proclamation

Nobbie's interest in this story increased when Lizzie the Lizard began to creep up on the policeman. When Lizzie slithered up on the table near to the officer's revolver, he stopped me reading and said, "A policeman would keep his gun in his belt." At the end of the story he wanted the same kind of gun. When I asked what he would do with it, he said, "I'll scare my friends and then we'll all have some."

Well, Choongko, my boy, it's a long time since I've sent you a story but it is because I haven't been well. I hear that you are learning to print and to write. I was very much impressed with that piece of paper that you sent with the writing on it. Always send me some writing.

Well, the story today is about the Club of course, although next time I am going to tell you a story of my grandfather, your great-grandfather, that is. Your mommy will explain to you about the meaning of grandfather and great-grandfather. I am going to tell you a story about him next time. But this time it's a story about the Club.

Christmas was coming near and the Club used to celebrate Christmas because, well, everybody celebrated Christmas and they said we might as well celebrate too. So there was a meeting one day in the Club. And it was a big meeting. Everybody was there except one or two. Big Bruno had sent out a circular to everybody to say that they had to come to the meeting. Big Bruno was in the chair and then there was Storky the Stork. There was Tim the Eagle. There was Philbert and Flibert the Fleas. Lizzie the Lizard. There was Tweet-Tweet the Bird. There was Leo the Lion. He had a toothache but he was there doing his best not to make a noise. Moby Dick sent to say that he was in the harbor, and if they wanted him, they just had to send to tell him what they wanted, because he couldn't come. It was too hard for him to climb up on the pier and go through the streets. But he was near there. Everybody was there except Peter the Painter. Bad Boo-boo-loo was there, and Good Boongko. They were holding their meeting to decide what form the Christmas celebrations should take. So the meeting was going on and there was a lot of talking. And Bad Boo-boo-loo wasn't saying very much. It was very strange for him, because he was always talking. And they thought that somebody should write a play so that they could have a play at Christmas and they could charge for people to come in when suddenly there was a knock at the door, a heavy knock like a piece of wood striking the door. Everybody was startled. Big Bruno said, "Good Boongko, go to the door please, and see who is there. We don't want anybody disturbing our meeting. Sounds like a cop." So Good Boongko went to the door, and when he opened it, there was a cop standing at the door.

He was a most ferocious looking cop. He had a tremendous mustache and a revolver case in his belt and the head of a revolver sticking out of it and he had on a sword and a big billy stick and he had a lot of medals on his jacket, and in his hand he held an official-looking paper. He came marching right in when Good Boongko opened the door, and before Good Boongko asked what he wanted, he pushed right in. And there was a table by the door and he knocked his billy stick on the table and then he pulled out his revolver from the revolver case and put it on the table.

Everybody in the Club was watching him and wondering what was going on. So he said, "Listen please to this proclamation from the rulers of the town." Big Bruno in his big voice said, "What is it you want here?" The cop said, "You are Mr. Bruno, are you? Keep still now. Don't think because you are president that you are not going to do what I tell you. Everybody stand up." Big Bruno said, "Why should everybody stand up?" The cop answered, "Because I say so and it is the law." So they looked at his revolver and Big Bruno whispered to Leo the Lion, and Leo the Lion said, "Why I could jump from here and knock him over before he picks up that revolver." Big Bruno said to Leo, "You'd better not do that. Let us see. Let us stand up to hear what he has to say." And Big Bruno said, "All right club members, stand up."

The cop took out his paper and began to read. He said, "You members of this club have been meeting for a long time and you have been examined by the authorities and we have found that your behavior is seditious." Big Bruno said, "What nonsense is this? How is our behavior seditious?" Then Leo the Lion said, "What does *seditious* mean?" Good Boongko, who was a scholar said, "*Seditious* means when you are always plotting and doing things against the country and wish to overthrow it and put in another government." And the club members began to say, "But this is nonsense. We have never plotted against the government!" The cop picked up his stick and rapped it on the table. He said, "Quiet there! And let me continue to read the lawful legal proclamation of the authorities of this town." So Big Bruno said, "Let us hear him, let us hear him." The cop continued to read. He said, "In meeting after meeting, you have uttered seditious language." All the club members looked at each other.

Suddenly Good Boongko, out of the corner of his eye, caught a glimpse of Bad Boo-boo-loo sitting down behind a big armchair and his back was to the cop. Bad Boo-boo-loo was laughing so hard he could barely hold his head up.

Good Boongko at once suspected something because everybody was very serious but Bad Boo-boo-loo was laughing. So Good Boongko crept round to him and he sat down next to him and said, "Bad Boo-boo-loo, you rascal, you know what's behind this." And Bad Boo-boo-loo stopped laughing and said, "Me? How could you say such a thing?" Good Boongko told him, "Bad Boo-boo-loo, if you don't speak up, I will go to the cop and ask him if he has anything in that paper about you specially."

And Bad Boo-boo-loo said, "Go to the cop." But he said it in a peculiar way as if he was afraid. This time the cop was reading all the crimes they had committed and how they were going to be put into concentration camps and so forth. But Good Boongko went up to Big Bruno and said, "I believe Bad Boo-boo-loo had something to do with this." Big Bruno looked at Bad Boo-boo-loo and said, "I believe you are right." So the word passed around, whisper to whisper, that Bad Boo-boo-loo had something to do with this cop business. What to do?

Finally Lizzie the Lizard said, "I am going over there to find out how things are." So Lizzie the Lizard crept along by the side of the chairs and along the wall and climbed up behind the cop who was reading his terrible proclamation and didn't see what was going on. And then suddenly, they saw Lizzie the Lizard go onto the table and start eating the cop's revolver. He just was there gobbling it up. The cop didn't see what was happening but everybody started to laugh. And then, everybody rushed down to the cop. And Big Bruno looked at him and said, "You rascal. This is Peter the Painter. He is no cop." And then when they looked at him and pulled off his big moustache and everything, there was Peter the Painter. His revolver was made of chocolate; it was a chocolate revolver. And that is why Lizzie the Lizard had begun to eat it.

Everybody began to say this is a very fine joke, but where did you get this idea, Peter the Painter. And Peter the Painter said, "Well, to tell you the truth, it was Bad Boo-boo-loo who told me to come here and dress up as a cop and fool all of you." "That rascal," said Big Bruno, the chairman, "bring him here." But Choongko, when they went to call Bad Boo-boo-loo, he was gone. From the moment he saw Lizzie the Lizard eating the revolver that was lying on the table, he said to himself, "They are going to find me out and I'd better get home fast as I can."

So that is the story of Bad Boo-boo-loo and Peter the Painter at the meeting about Christmas.

OK, Choongko, now next time I am going to tell you the story of your great-grandfather and that is not a story of Bad Boo-boo-loo, but this must do for this time.

October 30, 1955, London

16. The Remarkable Greeks – Part 1

Nobbie interrupted my reading when we reached the second page where it was announced that a battle was to begin between the Greeks and the Persians. "Is it going to be a war?" he asked. "I don't want another story about bad men blowing up people with a big bomb." I explained that the Greeks and Persians didn't have bombs. I added that Bad Boo-boo-loo was sure to turn up and do something silly; didn't he want to know what it would be? That seemed to satisfy Nobbie; he had a particular liking for Boo and his antics.

Well my dear Choongko, it is a long time since we have had a story, but we are starting again. This time it is a story about the Greeks, a very famous people who lived many many centuries ago, and the story also concerns Bad Boo-boo-loo.

Now the Greeks were, perhaps, the most remarkable nation of people who ever lived. At least, that is what your daddy thinks, and many other people think so too. They built the most marvelous buildings. They made the most marvelous sculptures. They wrote books on all sorts of subjects. A great deal of the things you are going to study in school as you grow bigger, and even when you are a man, you will find in time it was the Greeks who first thought about them and arranged them and organized them. But the thing I like most of all about the Greeks was that they invented democracy. Everybody, or nearly everybody, was free to say what he liked and to argue any points that came up. Now the Greeks had as enemies the Persians. Chungko my boy, those Persians were awful, just awful. One man was boss of the Persians and everybody else had to listen to what he said, and when you went into his presence, you had to go flat down and bow your head down on the floor. Now the Persians hated the Greeks because the Greeks were democrats and wrote and talked about whatever they liked; and the Greeks hated the Persians because the Persians hated democracy, and believed in tyranny and oppression. By the way, Choongko, all this is quite true you know, and when I see you, I will tell you all about the Greeks and Persians and show you pictures of them and about what took place, and so on. So the Persians decided that they had had enough of these Greeks who used to talk freely and walk about freely as they liked. And they decided to send a big army and wipe them off the face of the earth. Choongko boy, in some of the greatest battles the world has ever known, the Greeks defeated the Persians and routed them so that they never turned up again to destroy democracy in Greece. One day I will tell you some more about those battles. They are some of the most famous battles in the history of the world.

Now the Greeks had a religion. Lots of different people have different religions, and the Greeks used to worship a lot of gods, and one of them was Apollo. The Greeks said that he and the other gods lived on the top of a very high mountain, and Apollo was the god who saw after learning and knowledge and all fine educational things. For example, if you had been a little Greek boy and were having difficulties in reading or writing, you would say some prayers to Apollo, and Apollo was supposed to help you.

Well about Apollo! I do not believe there was any such person, although the Greeks firmly believed it. And they built a temple to Apollo and this temple was in a place called Delphi, and nobody ever really saw Apollo. What is certain is that the priests of Apollo were there. Everybody could see them. They were always telling people they had just got messages from Apollo himself, and they made a lot of money, and this temple was very big and very rich and very famous. Particularly the priests of Apollo were rich.

Now when the Persians invaded Greece, they marched along a road that took them near to Delphi, where the big temple with all the money and all the precious things were, and Peter the Painter one day told the Club the story that he had read in a Greek history book of how the Temple of Apollo and all the money were saved from the Persians. This is the story that Peter the Painter told.

He said that when the Persians reached about one hundred yards from the temple, they saw lying on the grass a magnificent suit of gold armor, a very precious treasure. So the Persians stopped and looked at it and wondered how it got there. Then, while they were there, suddenly a thunderstorm broke out and rocks began to fall from the top of the mountains onto the Persians below. The Persians got scared. But the people who lived in Delphi, not the priests, were hiding up in the mountains. They started to come down from the mountains, and two warriors, three or four times the size of ordinary men, appeared from nowhere and started attacking the Persians. These mighty warriors were gods, and they beat the Persians so badly that the Persians turned and ran, and that is the way the temple and all the money and the riches of Apollo and Delphi were saved from the Persians.

Choongko my boy, as soon as Peter the Painter had finished the story that boy Bad Boo-boo-loo said, "I don't believe that story at all. In fact, I think it is a lot of nonsense. How did the gold armor get there all by itself, and what kind of warriors were these who were three or four times the size of ordinary men? Who ever saw such warriors?" And he said, "How did the rocks just suddenly start to fall down onto the Persians? A whole lot of fairy tales and nonsense." But Peter the Painter took out of his pocket a book. It was by a famous Greek historian called Herodotus, and he read it out exactly as he had told them. Bruno the Bulldog, who was in the chair, said in his deep voice, "The whole thing sounds very funny to me, but still, Peter the Painter has read it from the book." Bad Boo-boo-loo said, "I still don't believe it." So Storky the Stork asked him, "Well, what *do* you think happened?" "I don't know," said Bad Boo-boo-loo, "but I don't believe that." They asked him, "Well, what *do* you believe?" "I don't know," said Bad Boo-boo-loo again, "but I will find out," and he walked out of the Club very quickly because he was very near to crying. When Boo couldn't understand a problem but felt something was not quite right, he always had to fight back tears.

January 6, 1956, London

17. The Remarkable Greeks – Part 2

Nobbie was eager to hear the second part of the story about the Greeks because he wanted to know more about the suit of gold armor. The only gold he had ever seen was my wedding ring. He asked me to take it off so he could hold it in his hand. "Wouldn't a whole suit of gold be too heavy to wear?" he questioned. I couldn't think of an answer, so I suggested that maybe no one wore the suit; it was just put on display in a museum. And unlike Bad Boo-boo-loo Nobbie believed the story was true and wanted to hear if the bad boy could prove it was only a fairy story as he had claimed.

Bad Boo-boo-loo went home and his daddy saw him sitting in the corner with his chin on his hands for hours on end. And his daddy asked him, "What is troubling you, Boo?" And Boo told him. His daddy started to laugh and said to him, "Boo, you are quite right, it is a lot of nonsense. I shall tell you what happened." And this is the story that Bad Boo-boo-loo's daddy told him.

He said that when the Persians were coming, the priests were scared they would lose all their property and money, and they decided to abandon the Greek democracy and to make friends with the Persians. But the poor people who lived in Delphi were for the most part shepherds and were accustomed to taking their sheep up into the mountains. And on this day, they did not want to join with the Persians and betray the Greek democracy, so they went up into the mountains. Now, when nobody was looking, one of the priests of Delphi took the suit of armor out of the Delphi strongbox and put it out where the Persians could see it. That was to tell the Persians, "We, the priests of Delphi, are Greeks, but we are ready to be good friends with you and give you some nice treasure if you don't take all, but share it with us." You can imagine, Choongko, how Bad Boo-boo-loo's eyes began to dance as he heard this.

Boo's father continued and told him that the shepherds up in the mountains knew that there were huge rocks up there, and if a few men leaned against them heavily, these rocks would start to roll down the mountainside. They knew that because they used to feed their sheep up in the mountains every day. So as soon as the Persians reached a certain spot, the shepherds leaned against the rocks and down came the rocks, faster and faster. Now they were very huge rocks, and when they dropped among the Persians, they started to roll over them, and when the Persians ran one way to escape one rock, another rock was coming to the same place where he ran, and so the Persians got scared and started to run away. As soon as the shepherds saw that the Persians were scared and had started to run away, they came down from the hills and attacked them and drove them off with such vigor that they never came back even near to Delphi. "And that, my dear Boo," said Bad Boo-boo-loo's daddy, "is what happened at Delphi long long ago when the Persian tyranny was trying to destroy Greek democracy." "Ah-h-h-ha-" said Bad Boo-boo-loo, "now I am going to the Club, and I am going to squash that Peter the Painter with his Herodotus. But tell me, Daddy, what about the story of the two warriors who were so big. Peter the Painter read it out of the book." "Boo," said his daddy, "the priests were very much ashamed that they had been ready to betray the Greek democracy and join the Persians, while the poor shepherds had fought to defend the democracy." And he went on to tell Bad Boo-boo-loo that when it was all over, the priests had to say something to defend themselves, and they could read and write. So they made up this story about the gold suit of armor that got there by itself and how the warriors who were so big they defeated the Persians, and as they could read and write and the poor shepherds could not, that is how the story spread about among the Greeks and to Herodotus, the great Greek historian, who wrote it down.

Bad Boo-boo-loo was silent for a moment. "But, Daddy," he said, "Peter the Painter has his book, and I have no book to say what happened." "That is quite right," said his daddy, "but I have a book here which shows how some Greek scholars have studied Herodotus and shown that he was wrong on this matter. Here is the book and here is the page. But what are you going to do? You cannot read, Bad Boo-boo-loo." Boo said, "That doesn't matter, Good Boongko is going to read it for me." And Bad Boo-boo-loo went to the telephone and asked Bruno the Bulldog to call a meeting for next Saturday, when he was going to expose that foolish story that Peter the Painter had told them about the Greek god Apollo and the priests at Delphi.

Choongko, there was such a lot of excitement in the Club as you never saw. Everybody was anxiously waiting for Saturday to hear what that Bad Boo-boo-loo had to say.

January 6, 1956, London

18. Delphi and Herodotus Discussion

As we have seen, members of the Club are always included in the stories that are meant to teach Nobbie about the classics in literature and history. Nello was always stressing to Nobbie the importance of reading and writing. After a few years in America Nello was appalled by the ignorance and low level of literacy in the populace. He, of course, had had the advantage of a first-rate English education at the Queen's Royal College in Trinidad, and earlier from his father and mother. Nello's father was a schoolteacher and his mother a prolific reader of the classics. Then having been a teacher himself for a number of years, Nello knew that for children, history and such subjects must be made palatable and taught at a child's level of understanding. By including various members of the Club in adult subjects, particularly the obstreperous Bad Boo-boo-loo and his contrary outbursts, Nello kept Nobbie's interest at a peak.

So Choongko my boy, here we are again with the story of that meeting that Bad Boo-Boo-loo asked Big Bruno to call. As you remember, the meeting was about the question of the Persians and the Temple of Apollo at Delphi. Everybody was at the meeting, and even Moby Dick was outside in the harbor and had a little walkie-talkie (which Nicholas the Worker had fixed up for him) so as to be able to hear. Now Big Bruno explained in a few words what it was about and then he called upon Bad Boo-boo-loo to say what he had to say.

Boo was all dressed up in his gray suit and everybody knew that he was going to talk, but how astonished everyone was when he walked up with two or three large books under his arm and stood up at the desk where the speakers used to speak on special occasions – it is called a rostrum. Then began the most astonishing thing. It was not only that Bad Boo-boo-loo told the story that his father had told him and explained all about Herodotus and how the priests had spread the untrue stories to save their own faces, and how Herodotus had made a mistake in writing them down, Boo *actually read them out* from the books! He began by saying, "Now friends, as Professor Jackson has said," and then he would open the book and read away, and then he would say, "Another great modern traveler, Mr. Jones, has said," and then Boo would take up another book and turn the pages and read away. Choongko, the thing was terrific because Boo showed quite clearly that there was no need to believe in any big warriors who had come from the sky to fight for the Greeks, and he showed how the priests, not for the first time, had been ready to make a bargain with the Persians.

The thing went so well that when Bad Boo-boo-loo sat down there was great applause. Peter the Painter tried to argue and say that what Boo was saying was that Herodotus was no good as a historian, and that Herodotus was one of the greatest historians that ever lived. In fact, he was the man who invented history writing. But Peter could not get away with that, and Good Boongko, who you remember was a reader and a scholar, jumped up and said that Boo had never said that, and Boo, who knew as much about Herodotus as he knew about the moon but had a quick mind, jumped up and said, "Me say that Herodotus is not a great historian. Absurd. I believe Herobotus is one of the greatest historians that ever lived." Everything would have been all right if Boo had not called Herodotus "Herobotus."

However, just as things were looking good for Boo, Peter the Painter pulled out his book – another book – and he read a story, the story of Joshua; he said it was from the Bible. He said that Joshua was the leader of the Israelites (you remember I have told you the story of how David the leader of the Israelites squashed Goliath the leader of the Philistines). Now Peter the Painter read out how Joshua was leading the Israelites in a battle to capture the town of their enemies. And he called upon all the Israelites to shout and blow their trumpets, and when the Israelites shouted and blew on their trumpets, the walls fell down. The town of Jericho and everybody knew that story. Now Peter the Painter was a really crafty rascal because everyone knew that old Bruno, who was a great reader of the Bible, often used to read that story in the Club and sometimes they would sing a song about it, how Joshua fought the battle of Jericho (your mommy will teach you that song). When Peter the Painter told that story he turned triumphantly to Bad Boo-boo-loo and said, "Now Boo, if this story is a good story, why do you find it impossible to believe the story that Herodotus tells?"

Now Boo was in a bad way. It was all very well for Boo to come and talk a lot about what his father had told him, but between us Choongko, Boo did not know very much and now he was in a spot. But Nicholas the Worker came to his rescue.

Nicholas said, "Boo, you have a little point there, but it is not much. When I was a little boy, my father used to read that story to me from the Bible, and he and my mother and all of them used to believe it. Then later a lot of people used to say that the story was not true, that it was a ridiculous story, but I have been reading up about those things and the story is probably a very true story. Because we know today that if a lot of trumpets and horns, etc., make a lot of noise all together, it can shake down a wall. Sometimes if a man is blowing it very loudly, a picture will fall off the wall. So there is nothing too peculiar about the story of Joshua and the trumpets. The walls were probably very shaky, and when the Israelites shouted out loud and the trumpets blew, it caused a powerful vibration and the walls came down.

That ended it, Choongko. That ended it that afternoon. Peter had to confess that he was defeated, and Peter was a good fellow. He was very interested in having all sorts of dramatic pictures to paint and he was ready to make good friends with Boo, so when Big Bruno said the meeting was over, Peter the Painter came up to shake Boo's hand and to have a little discussion – what people call a post mortem. And then a very sad thing took place. Peter the Painter said to Boo, "That point that you raised about the shepherds, I would like to hear it again so as to study it over." Now Boo at once opened his book and began to read it out just as he had read it before. The only trouble was that he had picked up a different book that was about something else, and Peter the Painter looked over his shoulder and he saw that Boo was talking about one thing but reading about something else. Now Peter, who was not angry but a little sore over what had happened, told everybody to listen to Boo and that important point. When Boo finished, Peter took up the other book and began to read the same thing. Then everybody saw that Boo had not been reading at all. You know what that boy had done, Choongko? He had got Good Boongko to teach him what was in the book, word by word, and he had learnt it off by heart so as to be able to stand up there and hold forth as if he was reading. Bad Boo-boo-loo looked pretty foolish when that was exposed, but Big Bruno said, "Nobody is going to get angry with you for that Boo, because what matters are the facts you got from the book, and the facts were correct. The best thing I can advise you is to go and learn to read as fast as you can, so that you will not get into messes like this, but at any rate you proved your point in regard to the Temple of Apollo," and everybody said, "Yes, that is quite right, Bad Boo-boo-loo has done very well."

However, that night, when Boo told his mommy and daddy how the meeting had gone, he was not too triumphant. He felt that he had won the point, but that he really had to get down to it and study up his reading.

OK, Choongko, that is the story of the meeting. You must write and tell me about it, and I know your mommy will read for you the story of Joshua and the battle of Jericho, and if you want to know more about Herodotus, I can send you a book with some stories marked off because he is a very famous man and wrote a wonderful history.

February 1, 1956, London

19. Roundheads and Cavaliers

This is a sad little story because it inadvertently reveals the pain that Nello feels in not being with his son. It made Nobbie cry when I read the line, "When did you last see your father?" Later, Nobbie dictated a letter to me telling his father that our friend John, who was in the merchant marine, was taking a trip, but "he always comes back."

Hello Choongko,

I sent you a postcard the other day. It says, "And When Did You Last See Your Father?" It is a reproduction of a famous picture. You must know that three hundred years ago in England there was a great civil war. That is to say a war between one set of people in a country and another set of people in the same country. On one side was the king and the nobles, and they called themselves *Cavaliers*; and on the other side were the people, and they called themselves *Roundheads*. Now the Cavaliers used to dress very beautifully and they wore their hair long and were very aristocratic, but the Roundheads used to cut their hair very short in order to look as different from the Cavaliers as possible, and they used to dress in very plain clothes. They were for democracy. Well, the Roundheads won the war and they used to go around searching for Cavaliers in the big houses that the Cavaliers lived in. Now some of those houses were very big indeed, so big that a man could hide in one and you couldn't find him although you searched for a week. When you come, Mommy and we will go to see one of those big houses. And the picture shows what happened once when the Roundheads went to the castle of a Cavalier, to search for the father. The little boy stood up in front of them and they examined him. They asked him, "And when did you last see your father?" Now, if the little boy had said that he had seen him that morning, then it meant that his father was still hiding in the castle and the Roundheads would find him and take him off to prison and perhaps shoot him.

Now pictures have to be examined very closely, so let us examine this one. The little boy is standing up in his fine clothes, and as you can see, he is only quite a young boy. I don't know, but I don't think he is much older than you; and he stands up very straight and very brave. The man who is examining him is very serious because he is doing a very serious job. But he isn't cruel and fierce. Next to him is a real Roundhead with a funny hat, and he looks at the little boy in a very severe manner. On the other side of the man who is examining is another Roundhead who is leaning back in his chair with his hands on the table, and he is very unhappy that such a company of big men has to examine the little boy. But war is a very serious thing and it is their business to find out where the little boy's father is. Facing us in the picture is another Roundhead and he is unhappier still at having to force the little boy perhaps to betray his father. The most striking one of all is the soldier with his pike who is standing to see that everything is in order. He is a big rough soldier, but the little boy's sister is crying because she is going to be examined next. And the soldier who has his pike in one hand in order to prevent any disorder has put his arm round the little girl so that she should not feel so bad. In the other corner of the picture are the little boy's mother and his elder sister. And you can see from the mother's face that she is very scared that the little boy will make a bad answer and let them know that his father is not very far away.

I don't know exactly what the little boy said, Choongko, and when you come, we may go to the library and look up in the books and find out, but from the way that the little boy stands up there, I have a belief that he is going to say it is a long, long time since he saw his father. At any rate you will agree, I think, that it is a very interesting story that the picture tells.

There is a lot of fun in examining pictures. You tell me what you think the little boy said.

Say hello to your mommy for me.

February 20, 1956, London

20. Bad Boo-boo-loo Rides in a Horse Race

Cheating is wrong, but in this case, Boo learns a lesson. Although he wins a gold cup for riding a difficult horse, he gets the booby prize in the junior division. I'm not sure whether Boo feels remorse, but at least he attends a riding school for a year, sacrificing ice cream and candies. Most of all, Boo does not like being embarrassed, but remorse and embarrassment are two different things. We shall have to read more of the stories to find out whether Boo has really changed after this experience.

My dear Choongko,

How comes it my boy that I have not heard from you? However, I have a lot of news for you.

First of all, have you ever been on a horse? It is a fine thing to be able to ride a horse. Well, I have been somewhere during the last few days in the country, and at the place that I was staying, there were a lot of horses and a pony named Paul specially for little boys to ride. I looked at Paul and I got a strong impression that you would like him very much and that he would like you too. So that when you come, as part of our programme we are going to go to the country for a day or two and you will have a ride on Paul.

Now, isn't that something? You must tell me some of the things you would like to do, and I will tell you some of the things that I am preparing. We are going to have a fine time.

However, what I want to do today is to tell you the story of Bad Boo-boo-loo and his adventures as a rider of horses.

Now Bad Boo-boo-loo just could not ride. He had never been on a horse and he knew nothing about it. But you know what kind of a boy Bad Boo-boo-loo is. He just likes to talk anything that comes into his head. So one day there was a great competition for horse riding to come off in the town where Boo lived. There was a competition for grown-up people and a competition for little boys under ten, and also little girls. Now there was a little girl only five years of age who was a fine rider and who could gallop and jump over fences on horseback. Her photograph was in all the papers and everybody was talking about her. So Bad Boo-boo-loo said, "If that little girl can ride, I can ride too. I can do all that little girls can do, especially a little girl who is only five years old." His friends told him he should not speak like that, but Bad Boo-boo-loo got very obstinate and said he was going to ride in the competition and that he was going to win the prize from the little girl, and then, as usual when people talk too much, Boo lost his head and said, "I am going to win the prize from everybody." And that rash boy went and entered himself for the horse-riding competition.

But after he had done so, Boo began to get cold feet. He knew he had made a fool of himself. He went and asked Nicholas the Worker something about riding and Nicholas told him that it was not an easy business and needed a lot of practice, so Boo was more disturbed than ever. He did not know what to do.

So he went to his old friend Tweet-Tweet the Bird and asked him for some help because Tweet-Tweet was always flying all over the place and knew everything and everybody. So Tweet-Tweet said to him, "Well, Boo, you should not brag like that but I will see what I can do. I think I will be able to help you. I will go and talk to my friend Boong-Doong." Now Boong-Doong was big horse, a mighty powerful horse, and he could run and jump over fences as no horse ever could, but he was a very difficult horse to ride and only the best riders could stay on his back. He used to jump so high and run so fast. Now Tweet-Tweet and Boong-Doong were very good friends because when Boong wanted to have a sleep – he used to sleep a lot – Tweet would stay near and shoo away all the flies that used to come bothering Boong. Tweet-Tweet told Boong-Doong about the mess that Bad Boo-boo-loo had got himself into and he managed to persuade Boong to help. Boong said that on the day of the competition whenever anybody got on his back to ride he would throw him off at once, but if Boo came to ride him, he would behave very well and he would gallop very fast and jump all the fences and he would see to it that Boo did not fall off. He said that all Boo would have to do would be to keep still. He gave Tweet-Tweet very careful instructions.

Now Boo's heart was in his mouth but he knew that this was his only hope, so for days in advance he practiced just sitting still. It was very hard for him, and his mother and everybody else were astonished to see Boo just sitting still.

Well, the day of the big competition arrived and everybody was there to see it. Boo went to the grounds and stood in a corner all by himself, very nervous, but saying to himself all the time, "Boo, your only hope is to sit still." The various competitors came into the ring and there were some riding and jumping and then came the greatest competition of all, to ride Boong-Doong. Choongko, it was funny, and even Bad Boo-boo-loo had to laugh. There were a lot of great riders, but as soon as they got up on Boong, he just twisted himself this way or that way and down on the grass they went. And this, mind you, was the competition for the grownups. It seemed as if nobody was going to win the Gold Cup, which was the prize for riding Boong-Doong, and then Tweet-Tweet flew down to Boo and told him, "Go ahead Boo and remember to sit still." Now the thing was well organized. The plot was that Boo should not ask anybody anything but should merely go straight up and hold Boong-Doong by the bridle. Now that is ordinarily a very dangerous thing to do, especially in the bad mood that Boong seemed to be in. But Boong was a good sport, and when he gave his word, he always kept it. As soon as he saw Boo coming towards him, he turned round and held out his head and touched Boo's face and Boong rubbed his face on Boo's jacket.

You can imagine the sensation. Boo, although he was still frightened inside, said, "I am ready to ride Boong-Doong." Now all the officials said that this was impossible and that Bad Boo-boo-loo would be severely hurt. But there it was. Bad Boo-boo-loo and Boong-Doong were standing next to each other as thick as thieves and Boong-Doong seemed to be in a very good temper. "We cannot allow this," said the president. But Boo saw a chair near and he pushed the chair up to Boong-Doong; then he jumped up onto the chair, and before you knew where you were, he was on Boong's back. And before anybody could stop him, Boo went off to the starting place with Boong and they started to ride along the course. Choongko, it was terrific. Boong-Doong knew how to throw people off his back, but he knew also how to keep people on his back if only they would sit still. And Boo had learned to sit still. They raced along the track; they jumped over the fences. There was a broad sheet of water sixteen feet across and Boong jumped across with Boo on his back and Boo really thought he was going to tumble off on to his head, but Boong was a great horse. When he landed on the opposite side, he pulled himself back so that instead of going forward over Boon's head, Boo merely had a light shock, and after that they took every obstacle and Boo came in at the end having taken all the fences as the paper said, "in superb style."

I wish Choongko that I could end this story here, but I cannot do that because it would not be the truth.

There was a lot of clapping and rejoicing and photographing and so forth such as you never saw, and Boo was undoubtedly a great hero because he had won the big Gold Cup.

Then the president came up and said, "Clear the course now because we are going to have the jumping for the juniors." And everybody began to say that of course Boo, who rode so well among the grownups, would be sure to win the prize for the juniors and that he would beat the little girl who had been riding so well up to then. Well Choongko, Bad Boo-boo-loo was in a fine mess. He could not ride and he knew he could not ride, and Boong-Doong could not help him because the juniors rode ponies.

So first of all came the little girl. Her name was Patricia. She got on one of the ponies and she rode around in fine style because she had been practicing riding ever since she was three years old. Then some other kids did their riding and at last the president turned to Boo and said, "Well, Boo, you take your pony and go round, we all expect of course that it will be very easy for you."

Bad Boo-boo-loo had no alternative. He went up to a pony and they helped him up and he started off. Even before they reached the first fence, Boo was slipping sideways. Then he got scared, and letting the bridle fall from his hands, he held the pony round the neck. The pony wondered what peculiar kind of rider was on his back. At the first fence the pony refused to jump and turned sideways and went through the gate. When they reached the little water jump, the pony would not jump either and he went into the water with Boo hanging round his neck. The thing was a perfect scandal. At the next gate the pony stood up quite still and Boo fell off. The officials came and helped Boo back on to the pony's back but Boo failed again to jump over the gate. He fell off twice on the flat, and at the second water jump he was so scared that he jumped off the pony into the water and it was lucky that the water was only one foot deep. The final indignity came at the end of the contest for the juniors. There was always a prize given for the one who had ridden the best, and also a prize for the one who had made the most mistakes.

The president announced that the winner of the first prize was Patricia Blenheim – that was the girl's name – and that the winner of the last prize (the booby prize) was Bad Boo-boo-loo. There never had been such a peculiar prize giving. For the winner of the big Gold Cup for the riding of Boong-Doong was Bad Boo-boo-loo, and the winner of the booby prize for the worst riding was also Bad Boo-boo-loo. Nobody could understand it except Bad Boo-boo-loo, Boong-Doong, and Tweet-Tweet.

Anyway there was the Gold Cup on Boo's mantelpiece at home and everybody said, "Well, at any rate, Boo did win the cup, and maybe when it came to riding in the junior race, he was not feeling so well." But Boo knew better than that and he determined never to be caught in that trap again. So he saved up his money and twice a week he went off for riding lessons, to learn how to ride. Slowly and patiently he listened to his instructor, and he bought no sweets and ice cream because he wanted to be able to pay his riding fees, and he did learn to ride well.

In the next competition he rode again in the junior's contest and although the little girl beat him, Boo rode very well indeed after his year of hard work and everyone was satisfied.

So that is the story of Boo and the riding. I must not forget to tell you something else. Boong-Doong said he wanted to join the Club and so he became a member, and when people used to ask him how it was that Boo was able to ride him that day so well, Boong, who could keep a secret, used to laugh and say, "That boy Bad Boo-boo-loo rode me because he knew how to sit still."

Nobody could understand exactly what that meant, but Bad Boo-boo-loo, Boong-Doong, and Tweet-Tweet had many a good laugh at it when they were by themselves.

February 20, 1956, London

21. The Liverpool Cathedral

Nobbie's remarks about this story were to be expected. First, the idea that anyone aged seventy was still alive and working amazed him. His second comment was disbelief that the cathedral was incomplete and would take still another twenty years to finish. He, of course, was used to seeing American construction workers rapidly completing their jobs.

My dear Choongko,

I send you another picture of that cathedral in Liverpool, and I promised to tell you about cathedrals. When you and Mommy come visit, we will go and see some very famous cathedrals, big churches, which can hold thousands of people.

Now it is a funny thing that the most famous cathedrals in the world were built for the most part about seven hundred years ago. In those days everybody was very, very religious, and therefore they were able to build magnificent cathedrals to worship in, to go there and say prayers and sing religious songs and so on. But after a time people were not so religious after all and everybody agreed that the cathedrals they built were not nearly as good as the old ones. The old cathedrals had long columns with arches at the top and they seemed always to be going up to heaven. They have a peculiar name – Gothic.

About fifty years ago the people in Liverpool decided that they were going to try to build a cathedral. They asked a lot of architects to submit plans and they finally chose a plan by a young fellow – almost a boy. He was just about twenty-one years of age. His name was Giles Scott.

Well, he started building and he has built a marvelous cathedral. Our friend, Lyman Paine, who is an architect by profession, says that it is a very fine building indeed, and although I don't know anything about these things, I think it is very fine too, and a lot of people who study buildings say that it is a great building, so it has the unique distinction of being a modern cathedral that is able to compare with the old ones.

The architect who designed it is now over seventy years of age, but he is still there building away because this cathedral is not yet finished, although they have been building for fifty years, and they say it will take another twenty years to complete. The old man is seventy or more, but I hope he lives to ninety so as to see the cathedral finished.

ОК, Choongko.

February 20, 1956, London

The Liverpool Cathedral 63

22. Children in the Resistance

Nobbie and I were in London visiting Nello, when on October 23, 1956, students in Budapest, Hungary, held demonstrations demanding independence from the Soviet Union. Police fired at the students, and a fight began between the two opposing groups. Almost overnight, throughout Hungary, there was a countrywide uprising. Revolutionary workers' councils and local national committees were formed, and by October 30 revolution triumphed. But by November fresh Soviet troops and tanks surrounded the airports and Budapest. Premier Imre Nagy called for help from the West and the United Nations, but no help came. Heavy fighting continued for days, and a general strike paralyzed the country for several weeks. But Soviet might won out, and the revolt was crushed. Nello was filled with joy by the uprising against the Soviets, particularly about the formation of workers' councils. He had for many years advocated such councils in the United States where workers and management would be equals and sit down together to plan the functioning of a particular industry. He did not neglect Nobbie in his political enthusiasm but told him about the brave Hungarian children who joined the fight by lying down in front of tanks or stopped their progress by various means. On our return to the United States, this story was awaiting us. Nello begins this story with promises of treats and a recap of an earlier episode before linking the children of Hungary with children of other cultures who acted bravely. In London, since all our conversations were about Hungary, he may have felt that a less politically charged opening would be more appealing to his son.

My Dear Choongko,

Well, little boy, how are you? Not a word from you for such a long time. I hope you are well and also getting on well in school. Now for some news. I am preparing a box for you. A Christmas box. It will have a lot of things in it. All sorts of things. Some of the things you left here, or rather all of them, and some new ones for Christmas and the New Year. I don't know when it will come exactly; it will be a little late perhaps, but when it comes it will be great fun, and when you have taken everything out, you will have a beautiful box to put things in, or to travel with.

Now, Choongko. You remember when you and your mommy were here in London we talked all the time about Hungary and Poland? Well the Club heard about what was happening, and Big Bruno, who is a very wise man as chairman, said, "Now I propose, as all of us are feeling so good and happy, about what is happening in Europe, all of us at once go and do a lot of collecting for the Hungarians." When we come back, Bad Boo-boo-loo will give a speech about the role Hungarian children are playing in fighting for freedom. Everyone agreed. So they went off and collected a lot of money because everybody was willing to give, and the club members worked very hard. On the following Saturday afternoon they came up for the rest of the meeting, and now, my dear Choongko, that boy Good Boongko was a great strategist. You cannot catch that boy napping anyhow. He was always thinking ahead. During the week, especially in the early part of the week, there was a lot of news on the radio about what was happening in Hungary. Good Boongko listened to it, and being a great reader, he read some of the things that were in the papers and told Boo-boo-loo, "Boo," he said, "we have to change the second part of that speech." "But why?" said Boo. "It sounded fine and besides I learnt it all off and I don't want to have to learn another one." "Come over here with me," said Boongko, "and I will explain." So Boongko took Boo into a corner and whispered to him and took things out of papers and read some things to him, and Boo said, "Yes, yes, yes," and shook his head. And he and Boongko got very busy for the next few days.

So on the Saturday they got ready for the meeting. But just before Big Bruno called on Boo, Peter the Painter got up and said that they all knew, or at least all those that had been reading the papers knew that little boys in Hungary had been helping to destroy the tanks and fighting with the revolution, so he thought it would be a waste of time for Boo to get up and tell them what they already knew. But he had to admit he was wrong. Chungko, my boy, as soon as Peter the Painter was finished, Boo stood up and said, "Mr. Chairman. I am not going to say a word about the boys in Hungary." You should have seen the face of Peter the Painter, and everybody was surprised. "Go ahead," said Big Bruno, and Boo said, "Thank you Mr. Chairman." Boo stood and he began. And this is what he told them.

He said that in the last big war the Fascists and the Communists had overrun foreign countries and had established secret police and other cruel officials who examine you, and they had a habit of stopping you suddenly in the street to prevent resistance. You had to show all that you had in your pockets to see if you were carrying some message or if you had some address to give them a clue to the people they were searching for. People were carrying on in every country a powerful support for the freedom fighters. Messages had to be carried and these searches found them, and many things were found out that the resistance people wanted to hide.

"Let us now," said Boo, "take the case of what happened in the Far East." "The Japanese," said Boo, "were oppressing some people in a Far Eastern island and some Japanese soldiers were guarding a big block of houses and examining everybody who went in and out because they suspected that the big block of houses was a center of resistance, propaganda, and activity – and the houses *were* a big resistance center. So the resistance people outside tried sending some old people with messages, but as soon as the Japanese saw anybody going in more than once, they used to examine them and sometimes torture them in order to make them say who had given them the messages, and where they were going.

At last the situation became very serious, until one day one of the resistance people noticed that the little children used to be playing in the big yard under the very noses of the Japanese soldiers, and when they had finished playing, some of the children went inside and some went home and the soldiers didn't say anything. So the resistance people decided to give the messages to one of the little boys and he had the messages and went and played with the other little boys, and while they were playing, he slipped the message into the pocket of one of the other little boys who took it into the house, and so these kids used to take the messages under the very noses of the Japanese soldiers. And the Japanese were astonished to find that the resistance movement now began to expand and develop, and a lot of activity was going on and they could not find out about it, and as a matter of fact, towards the end of the war, all over the world where there are resistance movements, the children played a great part in the carrying of messages because the soldiers and the secret police never suspected that they were the ones who were doing this work.

Here Bad Boo-boo-loo paused, and he took a little squint at Peter the Painter, and Peter looked very miserable. "Now to conclude," said Boo. He had asked Good Boongko to put in some good words and he had learned them off in fine style and was having a great time up there. "Now to conclude," he repeated, and it sounded so fine that he said it again, "Now, as I said, to conclude," and Big Bruno who never stood any nonsense, said to him, "Stop telling us you are going to conclude and conclude Boo-boo-loo." "Yes, Mr. Chairman," said Boo. "As I was saying, now to con – ," and then he swallowed the words. "There was a little girl who was eight years of age, and one day the Japanese secret police caught her mother doing resistance work and rushed into her house. They tied the mother down and started to beat her and torture her to get her to tell them what she knew, and when the mother would not tell them, they tied the girl of eight down too and told the mother, 'We shall punish your daughter and that will make you tell.' But the little girl said, 'Mommy, you don't tell them anything and I won't tell them anything, and let them kill us but they will never find out.' And the mother said, 'My child, if that is the way you feel, we both of us will say nothing.' And after a time the Japanese secret police and the soldiers had to give up and leave them alone."

Hereupon Boo-boo-loo put his manuscript down and held himself up in order to make a grand finale. "And therefore," he said in a low, deep voice, as deep as he could make it, imitating his father, "I say in conclu – ." But then he remembered he had said this too often before, and he stopped. But Big Bruno, who was very kindly, said,

"Go ahead Boo, say 'in conclusion.'" And there was a great burst of laughter from everybody and Boo felt rather foolish, but then he said, "Anyway I have shown you that children are useful in war as well as geese and other animals." That was not exactly what Good Boongko had written down for him, but at any rate he made the point.

Well, Choongko I told you how Peter the Painter had told people he was going to squash Boo-boo-loo before the meeting, and if it had not been that Boongko, that levelheaded boy, had worked out a bright strategy, Boo would have been stranded.

But Peter the Painter was a good fellow, and he stood up and said that it was clear that not only had Boo made a good case but that he had prepared the case well and had done a very good job. "So," said Peter, "I here promise to paint three pictures and offer them to the Club for the raffle and the proceeds are to go to the Hungarian fund." Of course everyone was pleased at this and there was a great burst of merriment when Peter the Painter said, "That, Mr. Chairman, is what I say in conclusion."

OK, Choongko. At this point your Daddy comes to the conclusion in this story. So please write me a letter as soon as you can and get ready to receive the Christmas box. FINALLY, you must tell me now what you want a Boo-boo-loo story about next.

November 29, 1956, London

23. Ghana Independence

We met Kwame Nkrumah, who became prime minister of Ghana, in the United States when he attended a university in Pennsylvania. Nello called him Francis, (Nkrumah's English name) and was his close friend and mentor. Nello had for many years been involved in the struggle for African freedom. As early as the 1930s he had collaborated with George Padmore, in the International African Service Bureau, an organization fighting for African independence. Before becoming prime minister and afterward, Nkrumah often asked Nello to come to

Accra for political consultations. Once again, in this story Nello starts the tale with history and then introduces the Club and its activities. In an earlier story, the Club was very much interested in the Hungarians and their fight for independence against Soviet Union, so Nello decided to broaden the theme and include other such struggles for independence.

My dear Choongko,

I think I shall be away for two weeks, beginning next Friday, and I am going to Africa. So before I go, I want to send you a story about Bad Boo-boo-loo and Good Boongko. Of course, when I am in Africa, I shall send you postcards and things from there. The particular place I am going is to the Gold Coast, and I am going because they have invited me to a great celebration of independence.

The Gold Coast is a colony of Great Britain, that is to say, the British ruled them and told them what to do. But little by little the Gold Coast people have fought and demanded absolute freedom to govern themselves and do as they please, and that has been agreed upon.

The date is March 6th [1957], and many people from all parts of the world will be there. The Gold Coast people do not want to be called the Gold Coast any more. They are going to call themselves Ghana. What makes it very important is that they are the first African people in the British Empire who have won freedom. And they take the name of Ghana because although a lot of people used to say that Africans have always been backward and that is why African countries had to be colonized, it is not true, and there was a great civilization built by Africans many centuries ago in the very place where the Gold Coast is now, and it was called Ghana. So the Africans are calling the new independent state Ghana.

Among other things that Africans used to do extremely well was to make statues and other works of sculpture, and I will get some pictures of the work they used to do and send them to you.

Now for the story of Bad Boo-boo-loo and Good Boongko. I have news for you about them, Choongko. Bad Boo-boo-loo has learned to read. The thing happened very strangely. He used to fumble about with his reading book and he could read some simple sentences. But the fact is that Bad Boo-boo-loo was not interested in what the book said, and as you know, whenever he was in trouble, he would go to Good Boongko and Boongko would give him all the information that he needed, and sometimes Boongko would write it out for him, and Boo would learn it by heart and pretend to read it.

But this time the Club decided to have a competition by which everybody would tell some stories about the struggle for independence. The Club was very much interested, as you know, in the Hungarians and their struggle for independence against Russia, so Big Bruno said that the best thing to do was for everyone to come and tell a story about independence.

Now Good Boongko ordinarily would have helped Bad Boo-boo-loo. But Boongko's father and mother had to go to the seaside for a special journey and they took him with them.

Boo, therefore, was left stranded. His father was away on a journey too on his business, and Boo's mother said that she was tired of always reading a lot of books for Boo and it was time he learned to read. So Boo was in a real jam because he could see that when the Club met he would have nothing to say.

So he went to the library, almost in despair, and he asked the librarian if there were any books about the struggles for independence. The librarian said, yes, and gave him a book full of such stories. Boo went home and looked at the book.

And one of the stories was about George Washington. And Boo is a smart boy. Nobody can take *that* away from him. Boo said, "I am sure somebody is going to tell the story of George Washington and the struggle of the independence for America. And then when they do that I will have no story to tell."

So Boo looked at the book and he turned it over, and he saw pictures of a boy standing with an apple on his head, and a man standing a little way from him with a bow in his hand. Boo looked at the picture and he started to look at the print, and Choongko, this is a fact, before you knew where you were, Boo was busy reading.

Many of the words he did not know, but he just went on and on, and after an hour he went over it again and he knew that he had a good story to tell.

So on that Saturday afternoon they all assembled in the Club and sure as day, Peter the Painter, who was first on the list, told the story of George Washington and the fight for American independence. But some people were not very interested because they knew the story, though Peter gave a lot of details that they had not heard before, and then Bad Boo-boo-loo stood up.

He said, "I am going to deal with Switzerland and the story of William Tell." There was a gasp from everybody. Where had Boo got that story? And then Boo told the story.

It was a long time ago and men used to fight in those days with bows and arrows, and the people of Switzerland were struggling to be free from some tyrants who were oppressing them. One of their leaders was William Tell and the enemy captured him once.

The tyrant said to him, "I hear you are a great man with a bow and arrow." "I do my best," replied William Tell. "Well," said the tyrant, "I am going to give you a special job. I am going to bind your son against that tree and put an apple on his head and you have to stand over here and shoot at the apple. If you hit the apple I shall let you go free, but if you miss I shall continue to keep you prisoner."

I suppose, Choongko, the tyrant wanted people to think that he was not so bad after all, although this was a very cruel thing to do.

"Do you accept?" asked the tyrant. "I accept," said William Tell.

The guards took the little boy and tied him to the tree and put an apple on his head and William Tell stepped forward with his bow and two arrows. The little boy spoke to his father. He said, "Don't be afraid, Daddy. I am sure you are going to hit the apple. Aim at it and don't aim too high because you are afraid of hitting me. I am sure you will get it right."

William Tell felt very encouraged and he pulled the arrow to his heart. It flew straight and split the apple into two pieces.

Now the tyrant had felt pretty certain that William Tell, in order not to hit his son, would shoot too high. He had not expected that

William was such a great marksman and had such courage and nerve. As a matter of fact, it was clear that he never intended to let William go at all. But all the people around, even some of his own people, broke out into such jubilation and applause that he realized that he had made a mistake, and that for the time being, he would have to let William go.

"All right, William Tell," he said, "go on, but before you go, tell me why you had two arrows? I had only given you one chance." "I know that," said William, "but if I had missed and killed my son, that other arrow would have been for you, and you can be sure I would not have missed."

Everybody gasped at William's boldness, and he walked away. But the story spread among his fellow fighters. William became a great leader among them and was one of those who helped Switzerland to gain its independence.

Bad Boo-boo-loo told the story so well that everybody was pleased. However, Peter the Painter, as usual making jokes at Boo, said, "Oh, Good Boongko must have told him that story because Bad Boo-boo-loo cannot read." And then Boo did a strange thing. Afterwards he said he did not know how he did it.

Boo went over to the bookshelves in the Club, where there was a book on George Washington. He opened it, and with his heart pounding, he started to read. There were a lot of words he did not know and had never seen before, but what he did not make out he guessed, and usually he guessed right.

Before he had gone very far, Big Bruno said, "Enough, Boo, you have shown us that you can really read." And then Bruno made one of his rare jokes. He said, "Ahem, ahem, I think we can say that to-day we have seen Bad Boo-boo-loo win his own independence."

ok, Choongko, I hope you like the story. Send to tell me what you want the next story to be about.

Hello to Mommy and all my love,
Daddy

February 19, 1957, London

24. Sir Lancelot and the Tack

Many children knowledgeable about computers will find this story intriguing – about a machine that shows historical events. It may strike them as something like the Internet and make it possible for them to accept the premise as normal. Adults may marvel at Nello's ingenuity inventing such an object fifty years ago. But the real genius lies in placing Bad Boo-boo-loo as an active participant in King Arthur's court.

Dear Choongko,

That Nicholas the Worker was a clever man. He could work with his hands and work with his brains. In fact, he said when he got an idea, his hands seemed to know just what to do. Now Nicholas was always inventing and making different machines. One of his inventions was a time machine by which he could transfer people to all sorts of historical events. And I promise you, and I will keep my promise one day soon, to tell you the kind of historical events that Bad Boo-boo-loo and Good Boongko used to see on this type of machine. But that boy, Bad Boo-boo-loo, was not satisfied with that. He always wanted to take part in the historical events themselves. So Bad Boo-boo-loo had a habit of looking at Nicholas the Worker's historical machine and then imagining that he was taking part, and when he would come outside, he would tell some stories about what had happened there and the part he had taken. And sometimes that boy would sit there and go off dreaming, and when he came back, it was impossible to tell what he had seen on the machine and what had actually happened to him.

This is what happened one day to Bad Boo-boo-loo when he sat all day alone looking into Nicholas's machine. Nicholas's machine was telling the story of King Arthur. There was an oath that the Knights of the Round Table used to take. They would swear that they would be gentle to the weak and courageous with the strong; that they would be terrible to wicked and evil people; that they would defend helpless people and a whole lot of things like that. They all promised to be very good. And in order to help them to be very good, Merlin the Magician, the man who had helped Arthur to become king (that is another story I will tell you another time), had a marvelous system by which all the knights, whenever they came to sit at the table, used to find their names in letters of gold on a chair. As soon as a knight was elected to become a member of the Knights of the Round Table and he came there, there on the chair, on the back of the chair when he was getting near to it and on the seat of the chair when he sat upon it, was his name. So all the knights used to come in and they used to have meetings and discussions to decide how they were going to help the poor and how they were going to fight against evil, and everybody used to go and take his correct seat. But Merlin the Magician was very curious also. And he made a law, and he had fixed it up around the table that if anybody sat on the wrong chair, he would be killed at once by the magic of the magician.

Merlin was not merely mischievous. But whenever a knight was rough with any weak person or was feeble in battle or did not treat helpless people with consideration, then Merlin would make it so he couldn't read properly and that is how the knight instead of going to sit in his own chair would go off to the wrong chair, and immediately, according to Merlin's magic, as soon as he sat on the chair, that fellow would be killed and fall under the table.

Now I don't know what was the cause of that. I don't know that it was so much magic. But Merlin was a great psychologist, and Merlin had got it into their heads, and King Arthur used to lecture them and teach them how they had to behave well. They didn't do too much reading in those days you know, and this reading of the names on the chairs was not so easy for them, particularly because Merlin used to have each chair in a different position for every meeting, and when a knight had done something wrong, he would be so upset and his mind would be so confused that he used to select the wrong chair, sit on it, and under the table he went. And after the meeting, some of the serfs (in those days there used to be serfs who did all the hard work) used to just pull him out and dump him in the same lake where there was a great sword. (That is another story I'll tell you one day.)

So it seems that one weekend Bad Boo-boo-loo found himself

there and was hiding behind a curtain, and he looked at all the names and saw the name of King Arthur there in letters that were twice as big as all the others, and Bad Boo-boo-loo thought that he would like to see and hear how a meeting went.

He heard the knights downstairs and Bad Boo-boo-loo went in front of a window because a curtain was just in front of the window. That's why there was a curtain there. And he looked round and saw the knights and there were a lot of them there. But there was a very big fellow, tall with a kind look on his face, and his name was Sir Lancelot. He looked up at the window and happened to see Bad Boo-boo-loo. And he gave him a smile and a wink and Bad Boo-boo-loo liked him at once. Then one or two of the other knights looked up at Bad Boo-boo-loo and they didn't like him very much, and there was one fellow in particular who called one of the serfs and pointed up at the window as if to say, "What is that rascal doing up there?" But Bad Boo-boo-loo was pretty smart. There were a whole lot of windows and each of them had a curtain and Bad Boo-boo-loo sneaked from a window on one side right round to a curtain for a window on the other side. And by the time the serfs came up to find out, they couldn't find anybody. Bad Boo-boo-loo escaped that time.

Anyway, Bad Boo-boo-loo stood up there waiting and suddenly the rest of the knights began to come in. First of all King Arthur came in and sat down on the big chair. And you know something, Choongko? He had a big mustache and a lot of hair, but aside from that he looked just like Good Boongko, if Good Boongko had grown up into a big man. Then the other knights came in and sat down, and at the end, this fellow came back in, Sir Lancelot. Bad Boo-boo-loo knew his name because as every knight came in, somebody standing at the door, the Lord Chamberlain, called out his name.

Now Sir Lancelot seemed very disturbed about something. And he seemed not to be watching what he was doing. He started walking over to the side of the table near where Bad Boo-boo-loo was hidden behind the curtain. Now there were two chairs there, and one had on it the name "Sir Lancelot" and the other had the name "Sir Gawain." And Lancelot was very preoccupied and he came and put his hand on the chair marked "Sir Gawain" and was about to sit on it. Bad Boo-boo-loo knew what was going to happen to him if he sat on the chair and he didn't want anything to happen to Sir Lancelot. He had just looked at him and liked him. And after all, Sir Lancelot, this big fighting man, had winked at Bad Boo-boo-loo. So Bad Boo-boo-loo was very scared that Sir Lancelot would sit on the chair and slip under the table and be dumped into the lake. So he said, "Pssst!" And when he did that, everybody turned round and Sir Lancelot turned round too. But it didn't save the situation very much because Sir Lancelot turned back and pulled the chair a little farther out. He was a very big fellow, you know, and all the chairs were the same size. All the knights had to squeeze into their chairs. Luckily, Bad Boo-boo-loo had in his pocket some tacks and a hammer that he had been playing with that afternoon, so he slipped out from the curtain and put a tack right on the seat where Sir Lancelot was going to sit.

Now Sir Lancelot wasn't wearing any armor, and he sat down, and Bad Boo-boo-loo was there hoping that he would sit on the tack. And sure he did and when he sat on it, he was a great knight and a fighter, he didn't scream, but he jumped up very fast and pushed the chair away and stuck his hand to his fanny, and there was a tack and he pulled it out. And then he turned round and looked at the chair and suddenly the trouble that was in his mind passed away from him and he realized that he had been about to sit on the chair of Sir Gawain, which, if he had done so, would have meant he was a dead knight.

He pushed aside Sir Gawain's chair and rubbed his forehead and beat his head to get his brain clear. Then he looked at the next chair and saw "Sir Lancelot," his name. He sat down on the correct chair and realized how close he had been to dying.

Bad Boo-boo-loo listened to the meeting and the discussion and the great battles they proposed to fight, and he was very happy to see Sir Lancelot taking part and organizing with King Arthur. But Choongko, the end of this story is very sad. Bad Boo-boo-loo, it seems, had got himself into such a dream looking at the machine that he had put a tack on the chair that Nicholas the Worker usually sat on. Everybody knew that was his chair. And when Nicholas came in, he went straight and sat on the chair and shouted out so loud, "What the deuce is this here?" And Bad Boo-boo-loo got up suddenly and realized that he had not been sitting with King Arthur and his Knights of the Round Table. He was sitting in Nicholas's room looking at the machine and had got himself mixed up in that story. But there was the tack. And he had put it on the chair of Nicholas. And Nicholas was very mad at him. But Bad Boo-boo-loo told Nicholas the truth. He said what had happened. And Nicholas said he would forgive him because it was a fine story, and that Bad Boo-boo-loo should write it down. And now Bad Boo-boo-loo was not only a reader, you remember, he was a writer. But at the same time, he went to Good Boongko and told him, and Boongko said it was a fine story, and they wrote it down together and it is from what they wrote down that I have got this copy and am able to send it to you. But exactly how I got the copy will have to wait for another time.

ок, Choongko.

May 3, 1957

25. Apollo

Bad Boo-boo-loo and even Good Boongko make the mistake of thinking they know it all. In Greek, such an attitude is called hubris. It means exaggerated pride or self-confidence. Such an attitude gets children in trouble, and adults too, when they don't know what they are talking about.

My dear Choongko,

How are you? And I would not say a single word about that letter which I am expecting from you. I am just waiting every day to get it, and if even it takes a little time, that is ок between you and me, my boy. I am sending you a Bad Boo-boo-loo story because I am going away for a few days. Along with the story I am sending you a picture.

It is a picture of an ancient Greek statue that now stands in a museum in Olympia, Greece, which is a little town away to the south of Greece. I saw the statue in 1954 and I have many pictures of it.

Now, it is a very famous statue and one of the most famous in the world; and in many museums, both in this world and in Bad Boo-boo-loo's world, there are pictures of it and casts made from it. Do you know what a cast is? The statue itself is in marble and there is a way by which you can use soft clay and put it around the marble and then take it off, and when it dries, you fill the hole with soft clay again and it comes out just like the statue, so that people who are not able to see the original can see the cast and have some idea of what it is like. It is not exactly the same you know, because nothing can substitute for the original that the sculptor himself worked on. But you can get a pretty good idea.

Well one day Bad Boo-boo-loo was reading away in a book about ancient Greeks. The teacher had been teaching them about the ancient Greeks, and Boo and Good Boongko and some of the other boys were reading all they could about it. These ancient Greeks were the most wonderful people who have ever lived. They were great writers, great builders of temples, great fighters, and very learned philosophers, and Boo and Boongko were reading away and exchanging notes.

So that Saturday afternoon they went over to the Club and there they found Peter the Painter talking about the painting and sculpture of the ancient people. Bad Boo-boo-loo had read that the statue was an old statue, and he and Good Boongko, who were always making jokes at Peter the Painter, who, to tell the truth, used to make jokes at them, started a long story of how many millions of people had seen the statue through the ages.

Everybody knew that the statue had been made about the year 450 BC. So Boo and Boongko calculated that if the statue had been made 450 years before the Christian era began, and then in addition we have had 1957 years AD, that is to say, in the period since Jesus Christ was born. If they added the two together it made it nearly 2,400 years old. Then they asked Peter the Painter, and everybody was listening about how many people he thought would see the statue every day. So Peter must have known what they were up to and he said, "Well, taking one day with another, perhaps 10,000 people saw it every year."

So the two boys sat down and multiplied 2,400 years by 10,000 people every year and they made 24,000,000, that is to say, 24 million people. Peter the Painter said, "You two are all wrong." Bad Boo-boo-loo said, "Now, Peter, please listen. You agree that the statue was made in 450 BC or thereabouts?" Peter said, "Yes." "You agree that from that time to today is about 2,400 years?" Peter again said, "Yes." "Now, Peter," said Boo, "you told us that you thought that perhaps 10,000 people would see that statue every day." "You asked me a question," said Peter the Painter, "and I replied to your question, and I agree I said ten thousand." Then Nob, Bad Boo-boo-loo was feeling very cocky, especially since he had learned to read so well, and he was smiling and grinning when he said, "Peter, you may be able to draw and paint but you are pretty weak in arithmetic, because if you multiply the 2,400 years by 10,000 you will get 24 million." And then Peter said, "You two, and particularly you, Bad Boo-boo-loo, are always bothering me. Once or twice you have got away with things, but this time I am going to finish up with you for a long time. This is the history of that statue. That statue was made in the year 450 BC or thereabouts, and it was put up at the top of the temple. It remained there for seven hundred years or more. It was the temple of the ancient Greeks who were pagans. Now the Christians became very numerous and powerful, growing steadily after Christ was born, and by about the year 400 AD Christianity had become the religion of the Roman emperor who ruled the world at that time. He was determined to finish up with the ancient Greek religions and he gave orders that all the pagan temples and statues should be destroyed.

The temple at Olympia, therefore, as most of the other temples everywhere, was destroyed, and the statues thrown to the ground.

By this time Bad Boo-boo-loo and Good Boongko began to realize that something was seriously wrong, but they could not say any-

Apollo 79

thing because they did not know what was wrong. Peter the Painter continued. He said, "The statues lay on the ground for a long time. Then little by little the ground there began to sink and a river, which was near, began to bring water and sand to cover the ground where the temple was. So little by little the statues were covered over and lay buried beneath the ground for well over a thousand years."

By this time Choongko, Boo and Boongko did not know where to look. They felt embarrassed. "They remained there," said Peter, "and nobody knew anything about them. There were accounts of them in ancient Greek books, but people thought they had been destroyed. However, about seventy-five years ago, some Germans who were archaeologists, that is to say they go and dig to find out about old cities, started digging around the temple, and to their surprise they found bits and pieces of a whole mass of statues that used to decorate the temple, and they found this statue of Apollo, nearly all of him. They joined the pieces together and set him up in the museum with other statues. That is why we have him today. So you and all your talk of twenty-four hundred years is a whole lot of baloney, and although I can multiply as well as you can, and although the multiplication is correct, you have all the facts wrong."

Choongko, my boy, you never saw two such humble birds as Bad Boo-boo-loo and Good Boongko. Everybody looked at them and they felt like crawling off and hiding themselves somewhere, but that boy Bad Boo-boo-loo is a boy whom it is difficult to put in a corner and keep him there all the time. You know what he did, Choongko? He said, "Peter, I am sure we are all very much obliged to you for this interesting and valuable information. Everybody here has gained a lot by it, and I shall continue to read about Greek sculpture with more interest than ever."

At that, even Big Bruno started to laugh (and as you know, Big Bruno does not laugh very much) and he and Peter the Painter and all of them agreed that Bad Boo-boo-loo had a tongue that might carry him far, but also quite easily could get him into trouble. They all laughed and were very merry about it.

So, Choongko, that is the true story of the statue of Apollo. I send you a picture and I hope it will interest you. If you want to hear more about the other statues in the temple at Olympia, tell me and I shall let you know what Bad Boo-boo-loo and Good Boongko read about it.

With lots of love,
Daddy

May 27, 1957, London

26. The Fossil Fight

This story makes it appear that Bad Boo-boo-loo and Good Boongko will never be friends again. It is their first serious disagreement. Unfortunately, either the sequel was lost or Nobbie's father forgot to finish it. The reader is left hanging, particularly when the ending does not indicate anything except another fight. We would like to have heard how the two boys made up their differences but can only guess.

Choongko, my boy,

As I told you last night on the phone, the news is bad. Bad Boo-boo-loo and Good Boongko have had a quarrel, a tremendous quarrel, and they are not speaking to each other. In fact, Bad Boo-boo-loo says he will never speak to Good Boongko again, and that peaceful little boy, Good Boongko is so angry that he has taken out of his bookcase all the books that Boo gave him as presents, put them in a box, and put the box under his bed. And what makes matters worse is that the whole club is split down the center, and even Big Bruno does not know what to do to keep the peace.

The whole thing started with an article in the public newspaper by a professor at the university. It seems that some archaeologists – that is to say, men who dig below the ground to find out the remains of how the people lived in the old days – had found a fossil, the bones of an ancient animal pressed flat.

So one of the archaeologists published a photograph and he said that these were ancient animals that lived many thousands of years ago before men lived in the world. Everybody was quite satisfied and they went to see the fossil.

It was a huge animal, some thirty feet tall, and the Club had a meeting and they said that someone should prepare a talk for the next Saturday afternoon to tell them about these animals of past times and the world before man lived in it. Everyone as usual said that when it came to something like that, the best person was Good Boongko because Boongko was a reader and a great one at gathering information, both from books and from asking teachers and professors and journalists.

So Boongko settled down, and night and morning he worked hard to prepare his talk. His mommy had to send him to bed every night because he was sitting up late working on what he had to say.

However, I have to say that he asked Boo one day to look up something for him at the library. They used to go to the library and ask the librarian for a book on "such and such," and the librarian would give it to them and they would read and copy out the information.

This time Boo said no he was busy. And he answered Good Boongko so abruptly that Boongko was a little disturbed about it, but he was so busy himself that he thought perhaps Boo was in a bad mood, and that was all there was to it.

On the Saturday afternoon everybody was there and Boongko got up and made his talk. Boongko said that these fossils showed how necessary it was to be careful in what you say about past times. He said that when you read books that had been written by ancient peoples, there was a lot of talk in them about dragons and huge and ferocious animals. All the modern people used to say for quite awhile that this was a lot of nonsense and we of the present day knew better. Then they discovered fossils of huge and ferocious animals, and today people realize that the ancient people were not so dumb after all, and when they talked about huge and ferocious animals that lived in bygone times, they had these animals in mind.

Now, Peter the Painter, who always liked to make funny jokes, got up and said that there had been an ancient world known as Atlantis, in which had lived many men and strange animals, but there had been a great shifting of the earth and this world had been overwhelmed by the sea, and mankind had had to start all over again. Peter the Painter was not serious. He had read this somewhere, and when he said this, it was only to tease Good Boongko. Boongko, however, took it in good part and said yes, he had heard those stories and had read about them. And a famous philosopher named Plato had told that story in one of this writings. How that boy Good Boongko knew all these things heaven only knows – so when he was finished the Club said that it was a fine talk and they asked Boongko to write an account of it and send it to the newspaper because every day the paper was talking a lot about fossils.

Good Boongko said yes he would, and he wrote the article and sent it to the children's section of the newspaper, and the editor published it. Good Boongko signed it, "G. Boongko, on behalf of the Saturday Club," and everybody was pleased.

Now this is where the trouble began.

Two days afterwards there appeared in the children's section of the public paper a violent article written against what Boongko had written. The article said that modern people had every reason to believe that there had been a society consisting of human beings and strange animals and that this society had been destroyed by a great earthquake that had shifted mountains and had caused the sea to flow in places where it had never been before.

The article went on to say that if an animal had died so many centuries ago it would rot and disappear and not become a fossil. An animal became a fossil only because it had been subjected to tremendous pressure from between two slabs of rock and that all the fossils showed that these animals had been overtaken by some great catastrophe and that is why they had been preserved.

The article continued to make the point that in the continent of South America high up on the mountains, there were buildings for which nobody could account. Nobody knew how they got there. Furthermore, up on those mountains there were lots of seashells that showed that at one time the sea had flowed up there or that what is now mountain had been flat ground near the sea and had been pushed up by some great earthquake that had altered the face of the earth.

The article concluded by saying that it would be a great mistake not to take all this into consideration when dealing with the great question of whether a society of men and animals had existed long before the one we know today.

Now you can understand that Good Boongko, who was a very conscientious boy, was very much disturbed, and he came to the Club and said that by writing what he had done in the name of the Club he had brought disgrace on it, that he had not known anything of what the new article in the paper had said, and that he would try to find out all that he could.

That afternoon, very serious, Good Boongko went to the library and showed the article to the librarian and asked if there were any books that could give him some information. The librarian said yes he had the books all put aside because during the past days another little boy had been coming and reading them all the time.

Now Boongko is an honest boy and was not suspicious, and he said, "That is very strange. Who is this little boy?" The librarian looked up and said, "There he is, coming in now," and Boonkgo saw Bad Boo-boo-loo rushing into the library with a lot of notebooks under his arm, and two pencils well sharpened. Good Boongko lost his temper. He should not have done that, it is true, but he had cause.

He said, "Boo, you mean to say you found out all this and did not tell us and went behind our backs and sent the article to the newspaper?" Boo was in a mess and did not know what to say, so he pointed to a sign in the library that said "Silence Please."

But Boongko was very angry. He said, "Boo, was it you?" All that Boo would do was to point to the sign in the library. Boongko raised his voice and said, "Boo, did you do that to us?"

He spoke so loud that some old man in the library looked up, frowning, and said, "Shhh . . . Shhh." Boongko turned and went outside but he stood on the steps of the library waiting for Boo. But

Boo is a sharp boy, and after awhile he crept out from the library, suspecting that Boongko would be there waiting for him. And sure enough he saw Boongko sitting on the steps, his face like a storm about to break.

So Boo went back into the library. After another while he took a little peep, but Boongko was still sitting there. Now Boo began to feel very bothered. The time came to close the library and the librarian said, "Everybody go home please." So Boo went downstairs into the washroom and climbed through the window and dropped down, hoping to escape from Boongko that way. But Boongko had moved from the front steps over to the side of the building where he could keep his eye on the front steps and on anybody who was trying to sneak out at the back, because the building had high walls.

When Boo dropped from the window, he started to run, but there was Boongko in the way. Now Boongko had been waiting for three hours, and by this time he was boiling. He held Boo by the collar and said, "You little traitor. Even if you had found out all of that, you should have told me. Now that you have learned to read, this is the way you behave. You remember all those times when you could not read and I used to help you out. And now look at what you have done."

All this time Boongko was holding Boo by the collar. Boo was saying, "Let me go. Let me go." And he pulled himself away. His shirt tore into pieces and it was a new shirt that Boo liked very much. He held on to Boongko and said, "I will tear *your* shirt," and the next thing both of them were fighting like mad on the pavement.

There, for the time being my dear Choongko, I have to stop, but I will give you some idea of what happened next. They were fighting on the pavement, and a man was passing and he stopped and parted them. "Why are you two little boys fighting?" he asked.

So both of them started to explain, and they started the quarrel again and talked about fossils and Atlantis and previous worlds and treachery and the Club and Big Bruno.

Finally the man said, "Look here, little boys, it is clear that you two are engaged in some sort of serious dispute. I am the manager of Children's Television, and tomorrow afternoon I will give each of you fifteen minutes to explain what this is all about to the public. If you accept this, will you stop fighting and go home?"

So they agreed and next, Choongko, I am going to tell you what happened when the two of them got on the Children's Television program.

I could give you a hint for now though. After they had argued a bit, they started fighting again!

With love,
Daddy

September 19, 1957, London

27. Bad Boo-boo-loo and the Shark Fight

When I read the title of this story, Nobbie said, "I don't want to hear it." His attitude surprised me, particularly since he liked stories about Bad Boo-boo-loo. "Why don't you want me to read it?" I asked. "I don't want to hear about sharks biting people's legs off or killing them," his lips were trembling. "Malcolm showed me a picture of some sharks in San Francisco. They had big sharp teeth and were chomping on the leg of a little boy." Fortunately, I always scanned each story before starting to read so I was able to reassure Nobbie that no one was going to be bitten, eaten, or killed.

So Choongko, as I was telling you in the letter, when I heard that you were going to the water for a holiday, it reminded me at once of an adventure that befell Bad Boo-boo-loo and Good Boongko one summer when they went on a holiday to the sea.

Now Boo was not a good swimmer. He could swim of course, but the real swimmer was Good Boongko, who used to move on top of the water like a little motorboat. But Boo was not the boy to let anyone beat him at anything too much, so after he had tried in vain to beat Good Boongko at swimming, he said to himself that he was going to specialize in diving. He learnt to hold his breath under water and, while Good Boongko was disporting himself on the top, would go diving down in the bottom of the sea. His parents warned him, but he was sometimes very obstinate and ill-behaved, and he continued with his diving. Luckily for him Good Boongko always used to keep an eye on what he was doing.

Well, one day they were out in the bay bathing, and as usual, Boo's father and mother were keeping an eye on him. (It was very wrong of him to do what he did and he was lucky to escape, but we will see.) They were out at the very end of the bay, and he was wearing a special mask that Nicholas the Worker was experimenting with. The mask had a small tank of oxygen or hydrogen, or something like that, but the whole point is that when you went down below you were not in any difficulties for air so that you could stay a long time without coming up.

Boo took a dive and the water was only about three or four feet deep, but when he went below, he suddenly saw a big sink or gulf down in the bottom of the water. He hesitated for a moment, but he was curious to see what was there and he plunged in. He was no sooner in than the water started to suck him down. Round and round he went and he could not prevent himself from going down. Suddenly he came to the bottom, and there was a big shark who looked at him and said, "What are you doing down here?" Strangely enough Boo was so glad to hear somebody speak that he was not surprised, and he replied boldly (for he was a bold boy, that Bad Boo boo-loo): "I am just looking around." Now this was the worst thing that he could have said. The shark was not a bad fellow, but at that time the sharks were carrying on a ferocious war with the octopi. They were fighting all over the ocean, and each side wanted to be master of the ocean. They had their fortresses, and their arms, and their positions, and this hole into which Boo had fallen was not a natural hole but one that the sharks had dug specially in order to hide their ammunition and weapons of war. They had dug it very near to the shore because nobody would think that the big sharks that traveled about all over the sea would come to a shallow little bay to hide all their war material. The commander in chief of the sharks – his name was General Sharkenhower – had given strict orders that the sharks were not to meddle with any human being and particularly little boys and girls bathing in the bay. He wanted everything kept very secret. So you can imagine that when Boo said, "Oh, I am just looking around," the shark got very suspicious and thought that he was a spy for the octopi.

So the shark said to himself: "I have to obey the orders of General Sharkenhower, and besides, I don't want to harm this little boy, but there he is and he says he is looking around. The best thing that I can do is to take him to GHQ (that is, general headquarters) and let them examine him there." So the shark knocked on the bottom of the sea and the door opened (they had everything well organized) and another shark came up. The first shark said, "See what I have found here. I am going to take him to GHQ. You act as sentry until I return."

Now Boo was beginning to get very scared indeed. He knew that GHQ meant general headquarters, but where could this be? However, he never lost his head in a crisis, and he listened closely to what the sharks were saying to one another and he got the word Hawaii. "God have mercy," he said, "they are going to take me to Hawaii." Then the shark said to him, "Give me your hand." and he set off with him going at a great rate.

But as I said, Boo did not lose his head. Although he had learned to read, as you know, he only knew some of the words of a code that Nicholas the Worker was working on. When you made one tap, it meant one thing. When you made two taps, it meant something else. If you made two sharp taps, it meant something else, but if you made two taps with a long interval, it meant something else, and so on. Day after day Nicholas the Worker used to be working on this code, and Boo was a boy with a good memory and he remembered some of the code. So, with the hand that was free, he started tapping out a message on the air helmet that he was wearing because he knew that Nicholas the Worker had arranged the helmet so that it could send radio and wireless taps a long way. He tapped out that a big fish had him. Boo did not know how to tap out the word *shark*, that was taking him through the sea to (he could not say Hawaii, but he said . . .)

an island off the coast of America, Pacific Ocean, guitar, grass skirt, dance. Boo said to himself that he would show them, and he was sure that Nicholas the Worker would be able to work it out. But as he was tapping away the shark asked him, "What are you doing, little boy?" But Boo was very bright. He said, "Ugh, bad toothache. Have to keep on tapping even if it hurts me very much." The shark looked at him a little suspiciously but he said nothing.

Nicholas the Worker had just come home from the factory and was having his lunch in a hurry. Suddenly the instrument in his room began to tap and Nicholas the Worker heard the message that Boo was sending to him. Now Nicholas was a man of great precision and promptness of action. He knew at once that they had to find Moby Dick because Moby Dick was the only one who could help Boo, who was in the toils of the big fish. However, how to find Moby who was down near the bottom of the sea? Nicholas the Worker called Tweet-Tweet the Bird, and told him to go and find Tim the Eagle at once. It was midday, and Tim was having a snooze high up in a tree on a precipice near the forest, but Tweet-Tweet found him and told him to go and find Moby Dick and to give Moby the message. (You see Choongko, when you are up in the air, you can see what is happening below the surface of the water.) So there it was. The shark sped along below the water with Boo, and up in the air Tim the Eagle was speeding along looking for Moby Dick in order to save the boy.

So that, Choongko, is the first installment of the serial story in two installments. The next installment will tell you what happened.

I hope you like it.

[August 19, 1955,] London

28. The Shark Fight – Second Installment

After Nobbie had been reassured that the story of the sharks would not entail any bloodshedding, and I'd read the first installment, he was eager to hear the outcome. For some reason he had a special fondness for Bad Boo-boo-loo and wanted to find out what would happen to him. Nobbie was a well-behaved child, and perhaps his interest in Boo was that he did things Nobbie might have liked to do. Or maybe it was that somehow Boo always got out of his various peccadilloes without harm. On the other hand, his other favorite character was Mighty Mouse – absolutely no relationship to Disney's Mickey. Mighty Mouse was good, a virtuous hero.

So there you are, Choongko! The shark is carrying along Bad Boo-boo-loo to GHQ of the shark army. He is taking him through the water at a terrific pace, and Tim the Eagle has set off to find Moby Dick, who is the only member of the Club who can help them.

The trouble was that the sea in that country was so big, as it is everywhere, that Tim the Eagle didn't know where to begin to look. Then Nicholas the Worker had a bright idea. He got down to his time machine and sent a message to Good Boongko, which Good Boongko got through a machine that Nicholas the Worker had given to him. He told Good Boongko what had happened to Bad Boo-boo-loo and where he suspected the headquarters of the shark army was. He told him too where Tim the Eagle was and told him also that he was in communication by special rays with Tim the Eagle and he asked Good Boongko if he could help in any way by making some calculations. Now Good Boongko was a boy who could read very well and could work out mathematics, although he was only a small boy. Good Boongko got out his map – a big map of that country.

By the way, do not think that that island Hawaii is the Hawaii that is in our Pacific Ocean! Not at all. That country was entirely different from our country, from our world. But now and then they called some of their countries and rivers and so on by the same names as we call ours. But they used to spell differently, because after all it was a different country. So while we spell our Hawaii, H A W A I I, they spelled theirs H A - Y.

So, as I said, Good Boongko got out his map, and he had a little box of instruments with rulers and compasses and squares and all sorts of things like that, and he set to work to calculate. He had a big sheet of yellow paper and some hard pencils, and he calculated where Ha-y was and where the shark GHQ was, and he looked in his book and found out how many miles an hour sharks usually travel, and then he thought that inasmuch as the shark was carrying Bad Boo-boo-loo, he would have to subtract a little because the shark would not be able to go so fast. Then there was a continent in the way, and he calculated how the shark would have to go round the land because he could not go through the continent. And after all these calculations, he made a diagram. Then he spoke to Nicholas the Worker, who had come hurrying over, and they calculated where Tim the Eagle was and how fast he could travel. Then he calculated the wind and how it was blowing, and it happened that the wind was blowing in a good direction so that it added to the speed of Tim the Eagle. So on the diagram he drew a line where Tim the Eagle would meet the shark if conditions remained stable. But as conditions rarely remain stable, he calculated a variation. That is to say, that if Tim the Eagle went a certain way at a certain pace, he should more or less meet the shark and Bad Boo-boo-loo. He calculated it to a variation of about twenty to thirty miles.

So Nicholas the Worker sent a message to Tim the Eagle and told him to aim at cutting off the shark with Bad Boo-boo-loo in such and such a place and to forget about Moby Dick for the time being. It was more important to know where Bad Boo-boo-loo was than to find Moby Dick. Besides he had thought of another plan!

So after sending off this message, Nicholas and Good Boongko ran down to the sea, and there they told some fish they knew that it was impossible to find Moby Dick by ordinary means, but would they please pass the word to all the fish they knew to get hold of Moby Dick and tell him to find himself as fast as possible on the very spot where Tim the Eagle was to cut off the shark and Bad Boo-boo-loo? Now fish are very funny, Choongko. There are so many of them that they pass a message normally as fast as radio, or almost. One fish just tells another fish and so on and – whoosh, the message has gone! So they found old Moby Dick and told him, and

Moby Dick set off. He said to himself, "That boy Bad Boo-boo-loo is always making trouble, but he is one of us after all and he has done some useful things."

So there were the three of them: Tim the Eagle in the air, the shark with Bad Boo-boo-loo, and Moby Dick. Good Boongko's calculations were wonderful because Tim the Eagle spotted the shark and Bad Boo-boo-loo down below the water at the exact spot that Good Boongko had calculated. Unfortunately, Moby Dick was not there at the time. He was a little behind, but Tim the Eagle followed the shark and kept on flapping his wings in a peculiar way and Moby Dick saw him as soon as he reached the spot. By this time they were not so far from the GHQ but Moby Dick was an old campaigner. You remember how he had squashed Captain Ahab? Now the thing was getting difficult because the headquarters was almost surrounded by sharks, as the word had been passed round that a shark was bringing a spy. So the whole battalion came out to see their friend.

Moby Dick had to work out very rapidly what he was going to do. Tim the Eagle was just above the top of the water there, waiting to see. He did not know what was going to happen, but he was mobilized, ready, and alert. And then Moby Dick worked out a great plan. He went down to the bottom of the sea and gathered his strength and came shooting up to the top, just below the shark with Bad Boo-boo-loo, and he brought them up on his back above the water into the air, as whales can do. And the shark suddenly found himself in the air on the whale's back with Bad Boo-boo-loo. Quick as a flash, Tim the Eagle saw what was up. He grabbed hold of Bad Boo-boo-loo from the shark, and the shark was so surprised at being out of the water that he could not make any sort of fight. So he fell back into the water. By the time the other sharks swam to him, Moby Dick was off and Tim the Eagle had Bad Boo-boo-loo in his claws and was carrying him back home.

The boy had a narrow escape, but that boy Bad Boo-boo-loo really was impossible. His mommy told him that he had caused a lot of excitement and anxiety and had made a lot of trouble for everybody, but all he said was, "You know, I wish I could swim as fast as that shark who was carrying me to GHQ under the water. It was a fine ride." When his Mommy heard this she was very much tempted to spank him, but she did not and instead packed him off to bed early.

OK, Choongko, next time I am going to tell you a story of Ulysses and the adventure that Bad Boo-boo-loo had with him.

[August 29, 1955,] London

29. Ulysses – A Great Hero

Nobbie liked this story very much and thought Ulysses was a real hero until we reached near the end. When Polythemus, who had only one eye, captured Ulysses and his men and they decided to blind him, Nobbie was repelled, especially since they used a burning stick. It took him several days to accept the horror, but he eventually said, "I guess Ulysses and his men would have died in the cave, that's why they did it."

Well, Choongko, here is a story about the great hero Ulysses.

Now, my dear Choongko, there are some great heroes who have become very famous, and whenever people want to talk about something special, they mention one of these heroes. Samson was a great hero; he was a strong man. Hercules was another great hero; he was not only very strong but he carried out a lot of very great deeds. I do not know if you remember we have talked about Hercules, and perhaps next time I will tell you a story about Bad Boo-boo-loo and how he imitated Hercules and worked out a big problem, but that would be for another time.

Now, among all the great heroes of the past there was a famous set that fought at the siege of Troy. You remember the siege of Troy and how the Greeks built a horse and hid some men in it and by this means got into the city? Another hero was Achilles, a great warrior, but he had that weakness in his heel. There was Agamemnon. The first thing about him is that he had a terrific name: A-GA-MEM-NON.

He was the king of men and the chief of the Greeks and maybe one day I will make a tape for you Choongko and tell you the stories of some of the Greek heroes, and particularly the story of Agamemnon and his daughter. Then there was another hero, Nestor. He was a very old man. He was very wise, and whenever there were discussions, everybody listened to what Nestor had to say because he had been around a long time; but between us, Choongko, a number of people then, and some of us now, believe that Nestor used to talk too much and was a very tiresome old man – but still he was a great hero. He was the man of wisdom and experience. Then there was the hero I am telling you about, Ulysses, and he was a smart one. He was a great warrior, but he was also very smart, my boy. He knew how to work out things. Well, after they had defeated the Trojans, the Greeks started off home, but it took Ulysses a long time before he got there, and these are some of the things that happened to him.

On the way from Troy to Greece there was one particular island on which there were some women. They would not get married and settle down, and they would not go to work. They were pretty bad but they could sing beautiful songs, and anybody who heard them used to go ashore. It was something like the Pied Piper – you remember when the rats and the children heard his pipe how they felt they had to go along because he promised them such wonderful things? Well, the song the sirens sang was the same kind of song. Anybody who heard their song always went ashore, but as soon as they reached the land, these women had everything arranged and they used to catch hold of them and make them do all the hard work and be servants, and so on and so forth. Now nobody had ever heard the song the sirens sang, because once you heard it you went on the island and you never escaped. Ulysses wanted to hear the song, but he was a careful man and did not want to run the risk of being caught on the island and having to do whatever these women wanted, so this is the plan he worked out. He told the sailors on his ship to stuff their ears with wax so that they could not hear. And then he told them to tie him to the mast very tightly with a lot of sailor's knots so that he could not possibly wriggle out, and he told them that whatever he said they were not to bother and pay no attention but were to row on and not stop. So the sailors stuffed up their ears with wax so they could not hear and bound Ulysses to the mast very tight and then Ulysses told them to go and row near to the island. His ears of course had no wax. So the women on the island when they saw the ship coming said, "There are some men coming whom we are going to get here," and they started to sing their songs. And when Ulysses heard those songs, he began to wish to go to the island and he called to the men to cut the ropes so that he could go, but the men had wax in their ears and just kept on rowing by. And when the sirens saw that the ship was passing, they sang more enticingly than ever. And Ulysses started saying how he wanted to go and they should cut the ropes, but the sailors, they were not hearing any songs so they just rowed on and after a time they were out of reach of the singing, and Ulysses was safe and yet he had heard the song of the sirens. The only man who had ever heard them and lived to tell the story. As for the sirens, they were pretty mad. Nobody knows exactly what happened but I would suspect that they started quarreling with one another and one said to the other, "You did not sing right," and the other one said, "You should have stopped singing long ago, you are too old," and still another, "You can't even carry a tune any more." And I think, Choongko, there must have been an awful row, and the whole thing was due to the fact that Ulysses was a very clever man.

Now I will tell you one more story about Ulysses. It concerns Ulysses and the giant Polythemus. Polythemus was a terrible and a very big giant and he lived in a cave, which also was on the way between Troy and Greece. Now Polythemus used to like to catch men and make them do what he wanted. Ulysses should have gone the straight road home but he always liked to find out what was happening, to seek adventure, so he and his men got caught by Polythemus, and Polythemus put them in that big cave and every night he used to lock them in with the animals; so there, Ulysses was in trouble again. He and the men were there locked up every night and in the day there sat Polythemus by the door and nobody could pass. In the morning Polythemus used to drive out the animals and in the evening he used to drive them back in again but Ulysses and the other men had to stay inside the cave.

So Ulysses got down to work on the problem. Now he was not only a man of brains, he was a brave soldier too, so the first thing they decided to do was to blind Polythemus who had this one big eye in the middle of his forehead.

Ulysses never asked anybody to do something he could not do himself, and that is the mark always of a real leader of men, so Ulysses and the men burnt a sharp stick in the fire until it was burning hot and then Ulysses rushed at Polythemus and stuck the stick in his eye, and Polythemus howled because he could not see anymore. But that did not help them very much. Polythemus closed the door quickly, and next morning when he opened it, he let all the animals pass out and he put his hands on their backs to see if anybody was riding them. Ulysses and company had hoped to escape this way but when they saw what Polythemus was doing they quickly jumped off the backs of the cows and the horses and so the animals went out, and they stayed in.

A pretty bad situation! But next morning Ulysses turned up with a new plan. Each man got hold of one of the big animals and held on to its belly, and when Polythemus came to let the animals out, he passed his hands over their backs, and because he felt nothing there, he thought the men were safe inside the cave, but all of them were holding on below and everybody escaped safely and so Ulysses and his men were able to get down to their ship and set off again for Greece.

OK, Choongko, those are two stories about Ulysses. If you like them, I will tell you some more. There is a movie made about him, and I am sure your mommy will take you to see it. I will go to see it too, and then we three can talk about it. But Ulysses was a very great hero, a very great hero indeed, and people remember him to this day.

[August 30, 1955,] London

30. Mighty Mouse and the Sinking Ship

This story is based on the sinking of the Titanic, a White Star ocean liner on its maiden voyage that struck an iceberg and sank, leaving over 1,500 people dead. Thanks to Mighty Mouse, Bad Boo-boo-loo, Good Boongko, and other members of the Club, the ship in this story is saved, and no one drowns or is injured.

This is a story, my dear Nob, of how Mighty Mouse called on Good Boongko and Bad Boo-boo-loo to help him in some work and how they were able to come to the rescue of Mighty Mouse. Yes sir, the great Mighty Mouse was always coming to the assistance of people, flying around in his long streaming cape. But this is the time when Mighty Mouse was in trouble.

Now what happened was this. There was a ship that sailed away with a lot of people across the ocean. The ship had started from France and it was going way out to China. But while it was going out, it got into a storm. Now you must know, Chungko, that it doesn't matter how strong a man can build a ship. If it gets into a real storm, that ship is going to be in trouble. Well sir, a real storm came, and the first thing the storm did was to blow away the radio apparatus of the ship so that it couldn't send any messages. And the next thing was the ship hit a big iceberg, a mighty big iceberg, and then the iceberg tore a big hole in the ship. And there, way out at sea, the ship was going down, and it had no radio to send messages. And, in addition, the storm had torn away the lifeboats. So the people on the ship, and there were many of them, were in a lot of trouble.

Now Mighty Mouse was flying about as usual, looking to see if there was anything that needed to be done. He heard the big noise when the iceberg hit the ship. And he decided to go to investigate. When he heard noise, he was just next to the place where Good Boongko and Bad Boo-boo-loo lived. In fact, they saw Mighty Mouse sailing past and they waved to him and he waved back because ever since the time they had helped Mighty Mouse to stop the flood in China, they had been good friends.

But just as Mighty Mouse was about to set off to find out what was happening to the ship and the iceberg, an atomic bomb went off. He was struck by an atomic ray. Some people were carrying on experiments with atomic bombs in the sea and this ray got away from them and it hit Mighty Mouse in the shoulder. Now that ray was strong enough to blow a whole city to pieces. It couldn't do much to Mighty Mouse, but when it hit him, it did knock him over. And he fell down in the grass near to Bad Boo-boo-loo and Good Boongko. He was in great pain. And all he could say was, "Bad Boo-boo-loo and Good Boongko, ship, iceberg, danger," and then the pain was so great that Mighty Mouse fainted.

Now that boy Bad Boo-boo-loo was always doing bad things, it was true. But Bad Boo-boo-loo said to himself, we just have to do something to help Mighty Mouse. He said, "Ship, danger, iceberg. What do you think that means, Good Boongko?" Now Good Boongko had read a lot of stories, and he said he had once read a story about a ship, which hit an iceberg, and perhaps that is what had happened again. What to do? And Bad Boo-boo-loo said, "Let us go and ask Nicholas the Worker because Nicholas will know." So off they ran as fast as they could, but before they left, they covered up Mighty Mouse with a blanket so he could rest a bit and nobody would trouble him. They ran to Nicholas the Worker and told him what had happened. So Nicholas said they must find out if any big ship is on the sea. So they went off to the wireless station and there they were told that a big ship had left for China and that it hadn't been heard from for some time.

"That is the ship," said Nicholas. "That is the ship that is in trouble." But where was the ship? They didn't know where it was and the ocean is a mighty big place. "There is only one thing to do now," said Good Boongko, "and that is to find Moby Dick, that old white whale." So they jumped into Nicholas's car and down they went to the bay, and they were lucky enough to see Moby Dick lying on top of the water enjoying the sun.

"Moby," Bad Boo-boo-loo said, "we are in trouble. We want to find a ship that hit an iceberg, and all the people aboard are in danger." "That is very easy for me," said Moby, in his big voice. "It wouldn't take me very long to find out, just wait here." And Moby Dick dashed off through the water.

Now, as you know, Nobbie, Moby was terribly fast in the water and Moby knew where all the icebergs were because he had dodged icebergs for many years in the past. So he had an idea where that iceberg was, and whoosh-whoosh-whoosh, he went through the water and sure enough he saw the iceberg and the ship sinking slowly and all the people on the deck without lifeboats. Now Moby Dick was a kindhearted old fellow if you treated him right and Moby said, "I have to move fast." And boy, he went through that water so fast that in a few minutes he was back where Bad Boo-boo-loo and Good Boongko and Nicholas the Worker were waiting and he told them what had happened.

"There is only one thing to do now," said Nicholas. "Let us gather together some boats and go to save the people. Moby will pull the boats."

Moby said, "That ship is sinking fast, we had better hurry." So they got busy and started to get boats from the harbor and tie them together with ropes to go to save the people. And Moby started to move, pulling the boats behind him, and he really worked hard, and Nicholas and Bad Boo-boo-loo and Good Boongko were there in the boats and they were going through the water very fast. But with all these boats Moby couldn't go so fast as before. "Can't you go a little faster, Moby," said Bad Boo-boo-loo. But Nicholas the Worker said, "Do not trouble Moby Dick, he is doing his best." Then after a little while they could see the ship in the distance. But Moby Dick said, "That ship is very low in the water. I wonder if we can make it in time." And Moby redoubled his efforts and he was going faster and faster but still the ship was sinking fast. Then suddenly a strange thing happened, my good Nobbie. There it was, the deck only a few feet away from the water, and it stopped sinking. Boy, that last five miles Moby covered at a rate that astonished everybody who heard about it afterwards.

But when they reached the ship, guess who was holding it up? It was our friend, Mighty Mouse. Mighty Mouse was not one to stay sick long, no, not him. He had slept a little in the park, but although his shoulder troubled him, he didn't let that stop him from going to help the stranded people. So while Moby Dick was pulling the boats, Mighty Mouse was sailing through the air with his cape streaming behind. So you see, my boy, Mighty Mouse is even faster than Moby Dick, especially when Moby is pulling a lot of boats.

ок, Chungko.

Undated, London

31. Moby Dick Fights a Strange Eagle

Nobbie came home from school one day bubbling with news. Two schoolmates, Alex and Dennis, had gotten into a fight. When I asked Nobbie what they had been fighting about, he said he didn't know. He was more interested in that Alex had gotten a black eye. I asked him what the teacher had done to stop the fight. He said she sent Alex to the school nurse and Dennis, who was not injured, to the washroom to clean up. The two boys had been best friends, and now the teacher separated them and made them sit on opposite sides of the room. Nobbie didn't think the boys would ever be friends again. I wrote Nello, telling him that the teacher had not handled the situation properly. After receiving my letter, he wrote the following story.

Hi, Choongko,

Your daddy has been very busy, my boy, but here is a story, a nice story that your mommy asked me to write.

One day during the summer, the Club was having a picnic by the sea. Everybody was there, except Tim the Eagle who was late, and old Moby Dick was near the shore having a good time too. All the club members were buying ice cream and giving it to Moby, and he was swallowing it down a whole big lot at a time. Suddenly there appeared in the sky an eagle. At first the club members thought it was their friend Tim. But when this eagle swooped closer, they saw he was a big bird with a sharp face and a sharp beak. Now, Tim had a kind face, so this was a stranger. As soon as he came closer, Tweet-Tweet the Bird said, "Ho, now for trouble. I know that eagle. His name is Baddy, and he does not like Moby Dick at all." Tweet-Tweet was right. That Baddy flew down and pecked at Moby Dick; and Moby Dick started to spout water at him, into his beak and into his eyes, and Baddy had to fly out of reach and then Baddy came back again and Moby Dick hit him such a tremendous blow with a big spout of water that he got dizzy. But Baddy was game and he came back and dodged the next spout of water and hit Moby Dick a great blow with his claws. Moby Dick began to bleed, and Baddy flew off for a bit, obviously preparing to fight some more a little later.

So Nicholas the Worker was horrified. He said, "We don't want Moby Dick to be fighting like this." So the Club held an emergency meeting on the spot, and Nicholas the Worker said that they had to stop these two from fighting. So they finally decided that Leo the Lion should swim out to Moby Dick and tell him that the Club was ready to have a conference between him and Baddy the Eagle. And Tweet-Tweet the Bird was to fly up to Baddy and tell Baddy that although he was not a member of the Club, they were ready to have a talk with him and Moby Dick in order to stop this foolish battle. And Leo the Lion jumped into the sea and Tweet-Tweet flew up into the air to talk to Baddy the Eagle. But by this time Moby Dick was so mad that he spouted some water at Leo the Lion, although to speak the truth, he didn't spout very much and he didn't spout it very hard. During this time Baddy told Tweet-Tweet, "You get away from here, you foolish little bird. I am going to teach that big donkey of a whale something." And in two shakes they started to fight again. This time, Nicholas the Worker became angry. He said, "Come on, boys, we are going to stop them."

Now on the beach there was a helicopter, which the Coast Guard needed to use when it traveled around. And Nicholas the Worker could fly a helicopter. So he and all the club members picked up a lot of sand on the shore and they piled into the helicopter. Up into the air went the helicopter, and Nicholas started to let out a lot of smoke around Baddy the Eagle. Baddy the Eagle was fast, but the helicopter was faster, and soon they had Baddy surrounded with so much smoke that he was ducking and dodging and couldn't see his way. Everybody in the helicopter was throwing sand at him and making him very uncomfortable. Moby Dick, when he saw this, started to laugh and said, "Bravo, club members, you are helping me. That's fine." But my dear Choongko, Moby was wrong. As soon as Nicholas had really made a mess of Baddy from the helicopter, he turned on Moby and gave him a good dose of smoke. Poor Moby was surprised and got angry and was looking to get some water to spout. But Nicholas the Worker kept dosing him with smoke, and soon poor Moby was sputtering all over the place and had to dive under the water. But as soon as he came up, there was Nicholas with some more smoke, and boy, Moby was in a bad way.

"Give them a chance now," said Nicholas the Worker and he flew the helicopter away. Then the Club agreed that Leo the Lion should swim out again to Moby and Tweet-Tweet should pay a visit of reconciliation to Baddy. By this time, these two big warriors after all their doses of smoke were so tame that they agreed to come and talk it over. Well, Nob, to cut a long story short, after they had talked it over, they decided to become friends. And before the picnic was over, Moby Dick was giving Baddy the Eagle rides on the water, Baddy sitting on Moby's head. It was very funny. Baddy applied to become a member of the Club, and he was accepted. Then Bad Boo-boo-loo said to himself, "Ha. This is really something. It seems that if two club members want to have a scrap, they can't because the Club is going to put a stop to that nonsense." He talked louder than he knew, for Nicholas the Worker heard him and said, "You are sure right, Bad Boo-boo-loo. This club is going to keep order whenever we have picnics and things." And that's the story, Choonk. I hope you like it and that Mommy likes it too.

Undated, London

32. The Monster in the Park

Someone at school gave Nobbie a photograph of Boris Karloff in costume for the film Frankenstein. *Although he shuddered each time he looked at the picture, he couldn't seem to put it away. A day or two later, he asked me to send the picture to his father and ask for a story about a monster. (Poor Boris Karloff, whom I met when I was an actress. He was a most gentle man, loved to garden, and discussed plants and flowers whenever we met.)*

Well, my dear Choongko, here our stories begin again. And if you send to tell me what you want a story about, I will always be able to send the stories regularly. Now you sent me a picture about a monster and that reminded me of a story about another monster and Bad Boo-boo-loo and Good Boongko.

Now one day Bad Boo-boo-loo (that boy who was always doing bad things) and Good Boongko said that they were going out for a walk in the park. So Bad Boo-boo-loo's Mommy said that as soon as it was dark they should come back home because everybody knew that as soon as it was getting dark the monster used to walk about in the park. Now he was a peculiar monster, very peculiar; if you did not trouble him, he did not trouble you. But if you troubled him, then he would get really mad and want to eat you up. So Bad Boo-boo-loo and Good Boongko said as soon as it was getting dark they would come straight home. So off they went. Well, they were playing a game of baseball, and they got tired and sat down. Then Good Boongko said, "It is time to go home, Bad Boo-boo-loo. You remember we promised to go home early." But Bad Boo-boo-loo (that boy who was always doing bad things) said, "Oh, I don't want to go home now. Let's stop here and talk." So Good Boongko wanted to have a little talk too, so he was weak and he gave in. (Oh, Choongko, it was a bad thing.) They sat down talking and then it became really dark and Good Boongko said, "Now, Bad Boo-boo-loo we just have to go now. We just have to go." But Bad Boo-boo-loo said, "Why?" Good Boongko said, "You know the monster goes around after it is dark." Bad Boo-boo-loo said, "But look. Look around, there is no monster. There is that gentleman over there and those two little boys over there and here is this tall man coming and look how he is smiling. He is no monster." And as a matter of fact, a very tall man with big shoulders came and sat on a bench near to Bad Boo-boo-loo and Good Boongko. So Good Boongko looked at him and saw that the man was smiling. And he said, "Well, little boys, how are you?" So Good Boongko and Bad Boo-boo-loo said, "Well, thank you, sir," because they were very polite little boys. And they went on arguing. Good Boongko said, "Let's go," and Bad Boo-boo-loo said, "No, we can wait a little bit. There is no monster, I tell you." So the gentleman sitting next to them said, "What is this about a monster?" and he was still smiling. So Bad Boo-boo-loo said, "Oh, we have to go in early because there is a monster that comes out after dark. But as you can see, sir, there is no monster anywhere." "Oh, no," said the gentleman smiling away, "there is no monster. Of course there is no monster." So Good Boongko and Bad Boo-boo-loo went on talking. But Bad Boo-boo-loo happened to look down at the feet of the gentleman quite by chance, and those feet were shaped very funny. And Bad Boo-boo-loo began to feel very uncomfortable because he had heard the description of the monster's feet, and although these feet were in boots, they were very peculiar boots because they had three tips for toes.

Now luckily Bad Boo-boo-loo was a boy who sometimes could keep his head very well. He did not get all excited. He remembered that there was one thing that could always defeat a monster. If you tickled him behind his ear with a piece of straw he used to collapse. That was his weakness. In fact that was his Heel of Achilles (and I will tell you the story of the heel of Achilles if you want to hear it). Anyway that was the monster's weakness. So Bad Boo-boo-loo whispered in the ear of Good Boongko. He said, "Good Boongko, do not get excited. Be calm. Now there is a piece of straw just over there on the path. I am going over for it, and meanwhile you talk to this gentleman. Ask him, 'What is the time?' or something like that." And then Bad Boo-boo-loo gave Good Boongko a little pinch on the arm. Now Good Boongko was a good boy, but he was a sharp boy too, and the moment that he heard what Bad Boo-boo-loo said he looked into his eyes and realized something was up. He started to talk to the gentleman, who was smiling all this time. He never stopped smiling until later and you will soon learn why. Bad Boo-boo-loo got up and dropped his handkerchief, and when he bent to pick it up, he picked up this piece of straw and then passed it down gently behind the gentleman's ears. Choongko, as soon as the straw touched the gentleman's ears, there appeared the most horrible face you ever saw. It was the monster, you know, but he had been smiling to fool people and then eat them. But when he felt the straw tickling his ear, he could not smile any more and you could see him as he really was. He stood up to catch hold of the boys. But the straw was tickling behind his ear and that was his weakness. He tried to stand up and then collapsed at the knees and tumbled flat down. Now Good Boongko thought that although the monster had collapsed, he would recover soon again. And as soon as he collapsed with his horrible face and his awful sharp protruding teeth, Bad Boo-boo-loo and Good Boongko ran for home as fast as they could. And so that time they escaped. But they had had a narrow shave from that monster. He was grinning at people to fool them so that later he could chew them up.

Oh, Choonko, if you want to hear the story of the Heel of Achilles, let me know and I will tell it to you.

Undated

33. The Babysitter

Nobbie had a friend, Natalia Barb, who lived in an apartment in our building. Whenever I left for a meeting, Natalia's mother would leave her daughter with my babysitter. The babysitter, Joanne, was a college student, and she and Nobbie got along very well. But whenever Natalia and Nobbie got together, they were impossible to handle, especially by one person. Something happened to both children, similar

personalities or some kind of chemistry. Whatever the cause the chil-
dren became excitable and unruly – utterly unmanageable. Joanne
came to me in tears and said she would look after Nobbie but not the
children together. I wrote to Nello about the problem, and he sent back
this story.

Well, Choongko, it is a long time I haven't sent you a story, boy. And
I hope you like this one very much. You know that Good Boongko
was a good boy and everybody liked him. But there was one occa-
sion, Nob, when Good Boongko was not a good boy. It was funny,
because as you and I know, Good Boongko used to listen to his
mommy and learned his lessons at school very well, and so on. But
there was one thing that Good Boongko used to do. Whenever his
mommy and daddy went out and left him with a babysitter, Good
Boongko just couldn't be a good boy any more. He didn't listen to
the babysitter. He didn't go to bed. He kept asking if he could go to
the bathroom. He would say that he wanted something to eat or
drink. My dear Choongko, I can't begin to tell you of the many ways
Good Boongko used to misbehave.

Now, everybody found it very strange because they said, "What is
it that makes Good Boongko unable to be a good boy and behave
himself properly when he has a babysitter." His daddy and mommy
would tell him, "Good Boongko," they would say, "you have to listen
to the babysitter as carefully as you listen to what we tell you. You
don't behave like that when we are here, why do you behave in this
way when the babysitter is here?" Good Boongko couldn't give any
answer. Then they would ask him, "Good Boongko, don't you like
the babysitter?" Good Boongko would say, "Yes, the babysitter is ok,
but I don't know why I behave in this way." So his mommy and
daddy tried to punish him, but it made no difference. Bruno the
Bulldog, had a talk with him and said, "Good Boongko, I could understand if Bad Boo-boo-loo behaved like that, that boy who is always doing bad things, but Bad Boo-boo-loo quite often behaves
badly with the babysitter, but then very often he behaves quite well

and we are all quite upset about it. But with you the thing continues all the time." Good Boongko would say, "Mommy and Daddy, I promise I will do my best." But it still went on and the babysitters were beginning to say they were getting quite tired of Good Boongko.

Well, one day, Good Boongko went for a walk in the park because the park was very near to his house, and he sat down behind a tree. After a little while some people came and sat down on the other side of the tree. And they began to talk. Good Boongko could hear what they were saying. The first lady said to the other one, "You know, Alice, I am very sorry for Jane." "Which Jane do you mean?" asked the other one. "Jane Simkins, of course," said the first lady. At this Good Boongko was startled because his babysitter was Jane Simkins. Then one of the ladies went on to say, "I am sorry for Jane because Jane has a lot of trouble. One of her children is ill and she herself is not very well. Yet she is a friend of the Boongkos, and when Mrs. Boongko wants to go out, Jane goes down to help them and also to make a little money. But Jane tells me that when she goes down there, that little boy whom they call Good Boongko behaves so awful that she is tired when she gets home and can't sleep, and she also says that when she is getting ready to go, she feels very unhappy because of all that that little boy does." The other lady said, "But then why does she go? She should stop going." The other one said, "No, she is a good friend of Mrs. Boongko and she doesn't want her to have to stay in all the time. But it is a shame that that little boy should cause so much trouble."

My dear, Nob, Good Boongko felt as if he wanted the earth to open and close him in. He felt so ashamed that he was causing so much trouble to someone who was only trying to help his mommy. And he felt ashamed also that people should be talking about him in this way. He made a resolution that nobody was going to say that sort of thing about him again. And after that, Good Boongko was the best boy you could imagine when the babysitter came, and very soon he heard Jane Simkins talking on the telephone one night and she told a friend of hers, "No, I can't go out with you on Friday.

Friday I am babysitting with Good Boongko and it is such a pleasure to babysit with that little boy nowadays that I wouldn't miss it for anything."

OK, Choonk. I sent you two books, and I'll send you another story next week.

Undated

34. Bruno the Bulldog Has Heart Pain

Nello called to tell me that he was having heart palpitations and might not be sending letters and stories as often. I was, of course, alarmed by the news, but he reassured me, saying that a specialist was looking after him and the condition was not serious. However, when this story arrived, I was even more worried. It was so out of character for him to show the fear that I sensed in the first part of this story. I couldn't decide whether he was more seriously ill than he had let on, or telling a story with a happy ending was his way of conquering a sense of foreboding.

Hi, Little Choongko. How are you little boy? I am still waiting for a letter from you. But here is another story. It is a story of Big Bruno the Bulldog.

It was bad, bad, Nob, but Big Bruno got very ill, and everyone was afraid that he was going to die. Now Big Bruno was the chairman of the Club, and all the members came to a meeting to decide how they could help Big Bruno. So Nicholas the Worker said that the only thing to do was to get a specialist. You know what a specialist is? He is a man who knows a great deal about one particular part of the body, and Big Bruno's heart was giving him trouble. He used to get violent palpitations. It looked very much as if very soon in one of those fits Big Bruno would die, and they would not see him anymore. So Nicholas said that they had to get a heart specialist. Then Peter the Painter said, no, to send for Mighty Mouse. So they sent a message to Mighty Mouse, and he came rushing through the air.

But Mighty Mouse said that if they wanted to travel somewhere or they wanted to build a big building or drive away some monsters, that was the sort of thing he could do. But when a man was ill, he could not get him better because he knew everything except human science.

Well, Nob, when they heard that, you could imagine how everybody was disturbed. So Nicholas insisted that the only thing to do was to find a specialist. Everybody agreed, particularly because the news came that Big Bruno had had another terrible palpitation and he had almost passed out. So they sent to find out who was the best heart specialist, and, Choongko, they found that he was a doctor who was spending his vacation in Turkey – you remember Turkey? So the thing to do was to get him. But the doctor's secretary said that he was very expensive, and it would cost ten thousand pieces of money to get him there. Lord, that was terrible!

Then Nicholas the Worker settled down to business. He asked Storky the Stork if he was ready to fly over to Turkey to get the doctor. Storky the Stork said he did not know if he could make it. But he said he could fly half the way and carry Tweet-Tweet on his back, and when he got tired, he would drop down in the sea and swim, and Tweet-Tweet could go on with the message. It was a long way and Tweet-Tweet had never had to take such a big flight before, but he said he would try it. Then the next thing was to get the doctor back at once. Now, old Moby Dick was off away on his vacation too. But Tweet-Tweet said that he would tell the sea gulls to look for Moby and tell him to come to Turkey to bring the doctor back.

So, inside five minutes, Storky the Stork went home and told his friends goodbye, and he and Tweet went off. Tweet-Tweet was a little nervous, but he said that the moment Storky got tired, he would fly off to get to the doctor in Turkey. He had the message tied to his leg. But in any case he knew what he had to say. As soon as they started Tweet-Tweet began looking for sea gulls and every time he saw a sea gull he told him, "Look for Moby Dick and tell all your friends to look for Moby Dick and tell him to go to the big harbor in Turkey. We want him."

Bruno the Bulldog Has Heart Pain 109

Then Nicholas said, "Members of the Club, we now have to raise ten thousand pieces of money. How are we going to do it? We can only hope that between Storky the Stork and Tweet-Tweet and the sea gulls and Moby Dick, we get the doctor here. But when the doctor comes we have to pay him." Everybody looked pretty glum, Choongko. Only Good Boongko got up and said, "I think I know a way to raise this money." Everybody said, "Speak up, Good Boongko." "OK," said Good Boongko, "this is what I think – ." And here, Choongko, I have to stop the story because it is a serial, and next week I will send to tell you what happened to this attempt of the Club to save the life of Big Bruno the Bulldog.

OK, Choonk.

Undated

35. Bruno the Bulldog Has Heart Pain – Continued

Today I'm going to finish off the story of Big Bruno and the operation. You remember the thing was to get all the money for the special doctor. Now to get all that money – well, Nicholas-the-Worker said, "We all have to go and do some special work – we'll just have to work to make that money."

Nicholas said he was going to a factory, and he was going to get work and work overtime and work on Sundays and so make a lot of dollars to pay the doctor, the specialist, who was going to cure Big Bruno. Then Leo the Lion said he would go to a circus and work in the circus for money and bring the money to help pay the specialist. Lizzie the Lizard said she knew where there were some fine potatoes in the forest. And if Peter the Painter would come and dig them up, they would be able to sell them and make a lot of money. Everybody said what they would do until it came to Bad Boo-boo-loo and Good Boongko.

So, Nob, here was a serious situation for Bad Boo-boo-loo and Good Boongko. They wanted to work to make some money, but they didn't know what to do because in that country children did not work. Bad Boo-boo-loo was very miserable, but Good Boongko jumped up and said, "Gentlemen." Then he continued, "Ladies and Gentlemen, give Bad Boo-boo-loo and me until tomorrow and we will tell you how we are going to work and make some money." So Nicholas the Worker said, "ok, we'll give you until tomorrow."

Bad Boo-boo-loo and Good Boongko started to walk home. Where were they going to get this money? So as they were walking along, they passed by the big library. You know what a library is. It is a place where there are a lot of books. Outside the library was a notice. Now Bad Boo-boo-loo and Good Boongko stood up and read the notice. The notice said, "Men and women wanted to help move books to the building next door. Ten dollars a day." Good Boongko said, "Bad Boo-boo-loo, look, they are paying ten dollars a day over there for moving books. But unfortunately it says they only want men and women and we are little boys."

As you know, Bad Boo-boo-loo was always doing bad things, but sometimes he used to do some things that turned out well. So it was just like him to say, "Oh, they say men but let us go see." Good Boongko told him again, "But we are boys!" But Bad Boo-boo-loo insisted and said, "Let's go talk to the man." So the boys went in and saw the chief of the library, who is called a librarian. And Bad Boo-boo-loo said to him, "Sir, we are here to work." The librarian said, "But you are little boys; you can't do a man's work." Bad Boo-boo-loo said, "If Good Boongko and I work together, we can carry as many books as a man. Two boys are equal to one man in work. So if you promise us the ten dollars we will work." "Go away," said the librarian, "you are too small." And then, my dear Choongko, Bad Boo-boo-loo did a strange thing. He pulled at Good Boongko and told him to come and went to where some men were working at the shelving of books. He picked up some books and told Good Boongko to pick up some, and both of them ran down the steps and they followed the men who were working into the house next door, and they put the books on the shelf and came back with the workers who were working. And Bad Boo-boo-loo said to the librarian, "Well, sir, you see how we can work." And the librarian said, "Go ahead."

Bruno the Bulldog Has Heart Pain – Continued 111

Well, my dear Choongko, Bad Boo-boo-loo and Good Boongko worked all day, and then they ran home, for this was during the holidays and there wasn't any school. They got up in the morning, and when their mommies thought they had gone to play, they were there carrying the books. Up and down the steps they carried those books until they were dropping from fatigue. But they made a lot of money.

Meanwhile, you remember, Storky the Stork had carried Tweet-Tweet halfway to Turkey. And then Tweet-Tweet went off by himself. It was a long way for poor Tweet-Tweet to fly, but he went and landed in Turkey and he saw the specialist. And the specialist said, yes, he was ready to go, but how was he to get there? And then a seagull was seen knocking at the window, and he told Tweet-Tweet that he had found Moby Dick and Moby was there waiting in the harbor. So Tweet-Tweet and the specialist got on Moby Dick's back, and Moby set off and he picked up Storky the Stork on the way and whoosh! – they were there.

By this time Big Bruno was in pretty bad shape but the specialist reached him in time to save him, and when they told the specialist, they didn't have all the money for his pay, the doctor said he would work on Big Bruno anyway. And he worked on Big Bruno, and soon Big Bruno began to get better because the specialist was a wonderful specialist. When he was finished, he said Big Bruno is OK now; he just needs to rest. Nicholas the Worker said, "We are sorry, specialist, but we don't have all the money. We will have to owe you some. We feel very much ashamed." But just when he said that, Bad Boo-boo-loo and Good Boongko came running in. They were waving a lot of dollars in their hands because they had worked day after day and they had got all the money. And when they counted it up, it was enough for the specialist. They paid him all the money, and he gave them back some and said they should have a fine feast and celebrate that Big Bruno was going to be well.

And that is what they did, Choongko my boy, and that was the first time Bad Boo-boo-loo and Good Boongko learned how to work hard for some money to help their president.

Undated

36. David and Goliath

This story from the Old Testament about a Philistine giant slain by David during the wars between the Philistines and the Israelites was one of Nobbie's favorites. He always seemed to be sympathetic to the smaller or weaker adversary. And because Goliath was described in some accounts as being about ten feet tall, David really won his admiration because he was small or of normal size and wore no heavy armor in the fight. He was also intrigued by the idea that an instrument such as a slingshot could down such a giant. Of course, he wanted us to immediately find something with which to make a slingshot.

Well, my dear Choongko, here we are after a long time starting off the stories again. This story is a story that Good Boongko read in the Bible. So Bad Boo-boo-loo who was sometimes lazy and wanted to watch, rather than read, asked Nicholas the Worker to please show him the story in the machine. You remember the machine where you can look and see and hear all sorts of stories? Nicholas turned on the machine and Bad Boo-boo-loo saw it. The story is the story of David and Goliath.

Now David was a boy, a young fellow. He was about fifteen years old, just like the David who is your babysitter. David used to play with a sling. The sling was made of string and a piece of wood. You used to put a stone in the sling and turn it round very fast in your hand and then let it go, and the stone used to fly as if it was a bullet from a gun. All the boys used to play with slingshots. But David was the best. He used to swing his sling and the stone would go to wherever he aimed it. He could watch an apple right at the top of a tree, aim his sling, and pick the apple just as if he were cutting it off with a pair of scissors. And when the boys had competitions, David always used to win the first prize. But to tell the truth, Choongko, David used to practice morning and afternoon. After school he used to be out in the forest or by the seashore aiming his sling and learning to make that stone go exactly where he wanted it to go. Sometimes his daddy used to tell him, "David, why don't you come and do your lessons instead of always playing with that sling?" And David was an obedient boy. He would come in and learn his lessons. But early in the morning he would be out there practicing with his slingshot.

Now David belonged to a nation of people called the Israelites. Just as you are a little American and you live in America, so David lived in Israel and he was an Israelite. The Israelites were good people. They used to work hard and they used to behave well. But next-door to them were some terrible people called the Philistines. They were really awful. They would not work hard.. They used to steal, and all they were concerned with was to get money and goods. Sometimes the children could not learn to read because the parents did not know how to read. My dear Nob, those Philistines were so awful that although this took place a long time ago, up to today when a person is really dumb and mean and cheap, people still call him a Philistine. Well the Philistines were always having quarrels and wars with the Israelites. In those days they sometimes fought a war in a peculiar way. One side would choose a great warrior and the other side would choose a great warrior, and these two would fight it out while all the others watched, and according to how it went, the war would be decided. If you ask me, that was a good way to fight wars and better than wars with atomic bombs. Anyway, the Philistines had a great warrior named Goliath. My dear Nob, he was terrific. He was big. He was eight feet, nine inches high, and whenever the Philistines and the Israelites had a war, Goliath used to be the champion of the Philistines. And he used to defeat every champion that the Israelites put forward. He had a great big sword and his arms were very long so that before the Israelite champion could get near to him he used to hit him a big whack on his neck and down on the ground the Israelite used to go, and Goliath used to put his foot on the Israelite's neck and the poor Israelites had lost the war again.

Because the Philistines had this big champion Goliath, they were constantly persecuting the Israelites and robbing them and behaving just like the lowdown Philistines that they were. The Israelites took it for a while, but then they said, "Well, we just have to fight them."

But the Israelites had no champion to fight against Goliath. Things looked pretty bad for them. Well, the day of the battle came, my dear Nob, and the Philistines sent the herald to say that Goliath was ready to fight anybody. The Israelites looked round for a champion, but no one wanted to come out and fight Goliath. And then suddenly young David came running up and said, "Let me go." So the Israelites said, "Little boy, go away from here. This is no time for jokes." And David's father was very angry and said, "Do you think Goliath is a bird or an apple for you to hit with a slingshot? Go home and study your books." But David said, "With my slingshot I can hit that Goliath before he gets near to me. Just look at this," and David picked up his slingshot and he swung it round and over and he let loose a stone. Now there was a little flag on the flap of a tent about fifty yards away and the stone went and it knocked the flag off the tent. David said, "If I can do that to the flag, I can do it to Goliath."

And the Israelite commander in chief said, "I believe you are right, David. I believe you can do it," and he called the Israelite herald and told him to come and tell the Philistines that they had a champion and he would be ready in five minutes. So the herald went and they blew some trumpets and the two armies stood up to see what was happening. And Goliath walked out in front of the Philistines with his tremendous big sword and his shield and his big helmet. To fight for the Israelites little David came out too.

David had nothing – no sword and no helmet. But he had some stones in a little bag attached to his belt and he had his slingshot tied round his waist. And when Goliath saw him, he started to laugh, "Ha! Ha! Ha!" That giant laughed and all the Philistines started to laugh too. But little David did not say anything, and then the herald blew the trumpet for them to begin and Goliath started to walk to David, intending to cut off his head with one stroke. But David just kept quiet and he unloosed his sling from around his waist and he took a stone from out of his little bag. David was absolutely sure that he was not going to miss. And when Goliath was about twenty yards from him, David swung his sling round and round, and he let loose the stone. It went straight to the temple of Goliath, and the big giant wobbled round and then tumbled over. He could not move because he was dead. And David walked up to him and took his big sword – it was nearly as big as David – and he put his foot on Goliath's neck, just as Goliath used to do to the Israelites.

Nob, it was a sensation, the Israelites let out a great shout of triumph and the Philistines turned and fled. They were scared and the Israelites ran after them and beat them and chased them away and it was a long, long time before the Philistines came back to trouble the Israelites again. Well, they made little David the commander of the army and the chief because he was such a grand fighter, and David lived to become a very great ruler of the Israelites.

And that is the story of David and Goliath. It is a very famous story and many great artists have made pictures and studies of David, and I will send you one next time. ok, Choongk, my boy. It is nice for stories to start again, isn't it?

Undated

37. Mighty Mouse to the Rescue – Again

Nobbie knew that we were opposed to wars; he had heard our discussions and in particular our alarm at the introduction of the atomic and hydrogen bombs. And to bring such principles to a child's level, Nello talked to him about people fighting. He told Nobbie that people should never fight unless they or their friends were attacked. The way to handle anger or disagreements was to talk. If agreement could not be reached, then the parties involved should just walk away, but never fight, never harm one another. But at the same time he told his son that if millions of people got together and were opposed, they had the right to try to stop a war.

Choongko, you remember that day when Bad Boo-boo-loo was using Nicholas the Worker's history machine and thought he had saved Sir Lancelot by putting a tack on his chair? Well, Nicholas was always experimenting and creating different machines. One day, Good Boongko and Bad Boo-boo-loo were in the workshop and were looking at one of Nicholas's inventions that he claimed could fly. One of the two boys wanted to try out this particular machine. The funny thing was that it was not Bad Boo-boo-loo who made the suggestion, but Good Boongko who said, "Let us go, Boo. I can handle this machine." Boo was quite scared but he didn't want it to show so he said, "Let's go."

Choongko, they rolled out the machine, which was built on a helicopter principle, and before they knew where they were, they had gotten inside, started it, and were zooming away into the air. Now the machine was beautifully made. Good Boongko had studied everything well, and though Bad Boo-boo-loo was not yet an expert in reading, once you showed him how to do something, he was pretty good. After about half an hour, Bad Boo-boo-loo was put in entire control of the machine, and Good Boongko began to read the charts and take notes. Everything was going fine when the machine started to slow down. "Good heavens," said Good Boongko, "I know what has happened. The machine is built to be a satellite. That is to say, to go round the world in the orbit of the circular movement of the atmosphere round it. Everything within a certain distance moves around as the earth moves round, and we needed no power. But as I read these instruments, I believe we went too near the edge of the orbit and we are now in outer space." "Outer space!" said Bad Boo-boo-loo. "We are in a bad way. We'll never get back home in time for tea, and my Mom is going to be quite angry."

Little by little the machine started to slow down. It was working on a special piece of the atomic-hydrogenic energy giver, but outer space was so cold that little by little the power was giving out.

"I don't want to start a panic," said Boongko, "but, Boo, we are in a bad way, and I'm sorry I brought you into this." But Boo said, "Boongko, what nonsense are you talking? You brought me into nothing, but if we are in outer space here and have no more power, the situation is bad. Good heavens, how I wish Mighty Mouse was near to us now."

At that moment, a calm voice said, "Here I am, you two adventurers. Don't you know that nobody comes into outer space without my knowing it? I knew you were in difficulties but I was about ten billion miles away unfixing a traffic jam between two stars, a comet, and a meteor. It was a mess, I can tell you. I fixed it up, but it made me a little late." Mighty Mouse was a very polite person and he added, "I am sorry for the little fright and inconvenience I may have caused you."

You can imagine, Choongko, how glad the two of the boys were. Mighty Mouse, who controlled more power than twenty times the power of any atomic-hydrogenic construction, guided the machine back into orbit and told them they would be home in half an hour. "In time for tea," he said to Bad Boo-boo-loo and smiled. Quite surprised, Bad Boo-boo-loo said, "How did you know that?" Mighty Mouse replied, "By my special radio-radar-television-total high-fidelity machines I can see and hear anything that is happening in outer space." They had almost reached home when Mighty Mouse said suddenly, "Listen to me you two. I want to give you a piece of advice and a message to Nicholas the Worker."

Mighty Mouse looked very grave and he continued, "This is the piece of advice. You two boys and the members of your club must work as hard as you can at studying satellites and missiles guided by the stars and so forth. There are some people on earth who are playing with these two things and preparing for war and they don't know what they are doing. We in outer space are frightened because at any time they can start a chain reaction of explosions that can destroy half the universe. We up here are on the alert, but we are asking people down below to study and to keep a watch. The situation is dangerous. And this is the message for Nicholas the Worker. Tell him that he must tell all the workers how dangerous the situation is, and they must get together to work out ways and means to put an end to this horrible armament competition that can so easily end in disaster." Mighty Mouse stopped speaking, and after a minute or two he said, "Well, here we are, in Nicholas the Worker's garden. I'll help you to push the machine back into the shed." When he had helped them, Mighty Mouse said goodbye and sailed away into the distance, leaving behind two very serious, very thoughtful, and very puzzled little boys.

OK, Choongk, that is the end of this story. Next week, I shall go on to another one. All my love to you and your mommy.

Yours,

Daddy

P.S. I almost forgot. When Bad Boo-boo-loo reached home, he found that his mother and father had gone into town and stayed for lunch so his mother didn't miss him. He was just in time for tea, however, and everything passed off well.

Undated, London